Follow My Leader

By JAMES B. GARFIELD

Illustrated by Don Sibley

SCHOLASTIC BOOK SERVICES
NEW YORK • TORONTO • LONDON • AUCKLAND • SYDNEY • TOKYO

To my daughter

CAROLYN

with love

ISBN: 0-590-09107-7
Copyright © 1957 by James B. Garfield. This edition is published
by Scholastic Book Services, a division of Scholastic Magazines,
Inc., by arrangement with The Viking Press, Inc.

23 22 21 20 19 18 17 16 15 14 13   0 1 2 3 4 5/8
Printed in the U.S.A.   01

ACKNOWLEDGMENT

Gold is valueless until mined, oil is useless at the bottom of the well, and my slight talent would not have found expression but for the eyes, the encouragement, and the helpfulness of Martha Frilling, to whom this grateful tribute is tendered.

Chapter
ONE

Jimmy Carter was sure the ball tipped the bat before it sailed past the catcher and hit the backstop, but Mike Adams dropped his bat and started for first base.

"That's a foul!" Chuck Wilson shouted as he ripped off his catcher's mask and snatched up the ball. "Come back here, Mike. That's a foul, I tell ya!"

Jimmy turned to the umpire. "What do you call it, Joe?"

Joe fidgeted. "I think it's a strike. The catcher didn't hold the ball, and Mike is safe on a third strike."

Chuck started to argue. The players dashed in from their places, all talking at once, giving their ideas on what had happened.

Chuck pointed at Mike and waved him back toward the batter's box, but Mike kept out of the argument. He sat down calmly on first base with a gesture that seemed to say he was there and meant to stay there.

"Play ball!" Joe shouted. The umpire was trying to regain his importance.

"I think it was a foul," Jimmy said finally, "but if Joe rules it was a strike there's nothing we can do about it."

"You bet you can't," shouted Mike. "You may be class

president at school, Jimmy Carter, but you don't run this ball game."

"Let it go, Jimmy," said Art Davis, who had come in from second base. "We can beat them anyhow."

"Not if Joe gives 'em the game," Chuck grumbled, returning to his position behind the plate.

"Batter up!" shouted the umpire, strutting a little now that his authority had been upheld.

Slats Anderson stepped up to the slab of cardboard that was home plate. He was thirteen — a little older and taller than the rest of the boys, and usually good for a hit.

"Take a lead," Slats called to Mike. "I'll bring you in. Run on anything, we're two out anyhow."

Jimmy stepped back into the box and calmly measured Slats for his first pitch. A little shorter than Slats, but tall and husky for his eleven years, Jimmy carried himself like an athlete. Standing there with his shoulders back and his head up, he looked like a rookie headed for the majors.

He checked the runner on first and wound up slowly, deliberately; then quickly flipped the ball over the plate with a sudden change of pace that caught the batter napping. Slats fanned at it, too late.

"Strike one!" Joe called, and Chuck threw the ball back to Jimmy.

Jimmy stood for a moment looking at Slats. The first ball had been a slow windup and quick delivery; now for a fast windup with a slight check before he delivered.

Slats had been caught napping on the first pitch, but he swung at this one before it reached him.

"Strike two!" The umpire was feeling his importance again.

Slats looked worried. Two strikes, two out, and a man on first with his team trailing 14 to 11. He decided to wait out the next one, and Jimmy put a sizzler right down the groove, cutting the plate.

"Strike three and out!" called Joe. Slats stood a moment, bewildered and a little angry, then dropped the bat and slouched out into the field with his team.

There were only eleven boys in the group. That made five on each team, with the odd man acting as umpire. When the bases were covered, there was no one left for the outfield.

Jimmy, Art, and Chuck sat together on the bench, waiting for their turns at bat.

"Good job on striking Slats out, Jimmy," Chuck said.

"Yeah, nice pitching," Art added.

Jimmy looked pleased. "I never told you fellows, but I want to play professional ball. Someday I hope to make the big league."

"I'll bet you make it, Jimmy," said Chuck. "You've got a good eye and a good arm, too."

Jimmy looked even more pleased, and was going to say something further about his ambitions when suddenly his glance fell on his wrist watch.

"Gee, I hate to break up the game," he exclaimed, "but I've got to get home."

"Aw, it's early yet," Art objected.

"Not for me," Jimmy told him. "Mom has to work all day since Dad died, and I've got things to do at home."

"Let your kid sister do 'em," said Chuck.

"Carolyn! Aw heck, what can she do?"

"You can play for a while, can't you?" Art persisted. "Have to give the other team their chance at bat, specially since we're ahead."

"Okay. I'll finish out this inning," Jimmy agreed.

They finished their half of the inning and then took the field. Again Slats faced Jimmy. This time he was not going to be caught napping. Jimmy laid down a straight one and Slats connected. The ball went out to left field, and they all stood and watched it go.

Art started after it from second base and Slats made the round of the bases, coming in for his home run.

There was a low place in the field that sloped down toward the side street, and the ball rolled downhill as Art chased it. Coming back, he ran toward them, waving something over his head. "Hey! Look what I found!"

The boys gathered around him.

"Where did you get it?" Jimmy asked.

"Found it over there in the corner where the fireworks stand was yesterday. Here, want to see it?" Art extended the giant firecracker toward Jimmy.

Jimmy took the firecracker and looked around the circle. "Let's light it," he suggested.

The boys stepped back as if it were a hand grenade.

"Not me," said Chuck. "I'm too young for the draft."

"It's too late," Art said. "This is the fifth of July, and anyhow it's against the law to shoot off firecrackers."

"Aw, it's just one firecracker," Jimmy argued. "What's the matter, you all chicken?"

"No, but it looks dangerous," Chuck said. "I think the fuse is too short."

"Golly, I didn't notice that. I guess you're right," Jimmy said.

"Maybe that's why they threw it away," said Art.

"Go on, light it, Jimmy!" Mike encouraged. "Let's see how loud it is."

"No, Mike," said Jimmy. "It's too dangerous with that short fuse."

"Aw, who's afraid of a firecracker! Let me have it." Mike took the giant firecracker from Jimmy's hands.

"I don't think you should, Mike," Art protested. "Kind of wish I'd left it where it was."

"Who's got a match?" Mike asked, digging in his pocket. "Oh, I've got one."

The boys scattered as Mike struck the match. "Look out for the demolition squad," he shouted.

"Don't *do* it, Mike!" Jimmy called sharply.

Mike touched the fuse with the lighted match, and as it sputtered, fear gripped him. He swung his arm in a wide arc, throwing the lighted firecracker from him. His attention had been attracted by Jimmy's voice, which caused him to hurl the firecracker unconsciously in the direction it came from.

Jimmy threw up his arms and tried to duck, but it was too late. The world exploded in a white flash. Deafening thunder smashed against his ears. Then the light was gone and the sound was gone. Everything became very dark, very quiet.

It was all over so quickly that none of the boys could explain afterward exactly what happened. For a stunned moment no one moved. Everyone stared in horror at the boy lying still on the ground. His face was blue from the smoke stain of the powder. His dark-brown hair was singed at the forehead. The boys moved toward him, moved slowly, uncertainly.

"Is — is he dead?" someone asked.

Chuck knelt down and put his ear close to Jimmy's chest. "No, he's breathing," he said with some relief.

"Better not touch him," Art warned. "Remember our first aid in Scouts. Who's got a coat?"

Slats came up with a sweater to put over Jimmy's chest.

"What — what'll we do?" someone asked.

"I'll get his aunt," Art called as he ran down the street.

No one noticed Mike as he stood apart from the group, his eyes full of horror. He wanted to run and hide, but he couldn't move. He just stood there looking at Jimmy. "I didn't mean to do it," he mumbled.

They all turned to stare at him. "Now look what you've done!" Slats said.

"But I didn't mean to do it," Mike repeated.

"We told you not to light it," Chuck accused. "Why did you have to throw it at Jimmy?"

"I didn't. It just went that way."

"You did too," Chuck insisted. "You threw it at him on purpose."

Mike's fear turned to anger. "I did not! Aw, dry up! Your mouth is leaking words."

"You ought to be ashamed." Slats started toward him.

Mike backed away. "Aw, go on," he called. "You've got the measles! You're a measly bunch!" He turned to leave, looked back at the grim faces of the group, and panic seized him. He started to run.

Jimmy's Aunt Martha lived only half a block away.

When Art told her Jimmy was hurt by a giant firecracker, she stopped just long enough to phone for an ambulance, then hurried with Art to the vacant lot, asking questions all the way.

The boys stood in awed silence when the ambulance drove up to take Jimmy and his aunt to the hospital. It was the first time that one of their Scout group had ridden in an ambulance. They felt a little important, but also very, very much afraid.

While Jimmy was in the operating room, Aunt Martha phoned his mother at her office and waited for her arrival. Mrs. Carter reached the hospital just as Jimmy was brought to his bed, his head wrapped in bandages, with only his nose and mouth showing.

Dr. Wallace and a nurse came down with him. Mrs. Carter hurried to the doctor. "How is he, Doctor? Please tell me the truth!"

"His face is badly burned, but I feel he is not in a critical condition," Dr. Wallace told her.

"May I stay with him?" she asked.

"That won't be necessary. There is nothing you could do, and while he's sleeping he won't even know you're here."

Aunt Martha came over to them and slipped her arm around Mrs. Carter. "You see, Doctor, my sister has been through this once before. Her husband died in an accident just a few years ago."

"But this is not that serious. Jimmy isn't going to die." The doctor smiled, walking with them to the door.

For the first few days Jimmy was allowed no visitors

except his mother and Aunt Martha. The hours dragged slowly; his only way of telling time was the radio with its earphone attachment, and the routine services of the floor nurses.

"And how is our mummified king today?" questioned Miss Moore, his favorite nurse, when she came into the room one morning.

"Very well, my Egyptian slave," he answered. "What offerings do you bring?"

"A delicious pill," she told him.

"I think I'll have your head cut off. I order nectar, and you bring me a pill."

"Of course. Egyptian kings didn't have nectar," Miss Moore explained. "That was the drink of the Greek gods. You know that."

"It's all Greek to me," Jimmy admitted. "Well, if I can't have nectar I'll take a glass of water, if you'll pour it for me. I spill it all over everything."

The nurse poured the water and gave it to Jimmy with a tube. The tube was like a soda-water straw made of glass, and it was bent so that Jimmy could drink through it while lying down without having to tilt the glass.

The days passed slowly. The powder-burned skin peeled off, and Jimmy's face healed unblemished, but his eyes were still bandaged, hiding the ugly scars around them. He was getting restless.

"I think I've played mummy long enough," he complained to Miss Moore one day. "When can I go home?"

"That's up to Dr. Wallace," she reminded him. "I think he's going to take a look at your eyes today."

"My eyes?" Jimmy questioned. "Why? Is anything

wrong with them? I thought my face was burned."

"Well, your eyes are in your face, aren't they? We'll see what the doctor says."

Aunt Martha and Mrs. Carter arrived at the hospital to be with Jimmy when the bandages were removed from his eyes. Dr. Wallace and Miss Moore came in with their usual cheerfulness. Jimmy heard the doctor's quiet conversation with his mother and Aunt Martha, but he couldn't understand what was said.

The doctor was telling Mrs. Carter, "I must warn you that the boy's eyes have been seriously damaged. We won't know how much until we see them."

"What do you mean, Doctor, damaged?"

"I won't say there is no hope, but we've done everything possible."

Mrs. Carter gasped. "You — mean he won't — see?"

"You must be prepared for that possibility," Dr. Wallace told her.

"He may be blind? Oh, no!" Her face was white.

"Let's wait and see, Ruth," Aunt Martha said quietly.

Jimmy heard the shades being pulled down, and Miss Moore coming over to him.

"Now young man, if you'll sit up I'll prop these pillows behind you." The nurse's voice was quiet, but Jimmy sensed an odd strain in her manner.

"All right, Jimmy," Dr. Wallace said. "I think we'll remove your 'mummy casing.' "

"Well, it's about time," said Jimmy. A surge of happiness started somewhere near his toes and came all the way up to his head, swelling as if to burst the bandages before the doctor could remove them.

"Hurry up, Doctor. I've got to see what's going on around here." Jimmy felt the doctor's hands at his head and the wrappings slowly unwinding; he was looking through the bandages, waiting for the first glorious burst of light. Layer by layer the gauze peeled off; then Dr. Wallace stopped, and Jimmy heard him step back.

"Go on, Doctor. Take off the rest of 'em." Jimmy reached up with his hands as if he would pull them off.

"They are off, Jimmy," the doctor said quietly.

"They're not off! I can't see!" Jimmy strained to look where his mother and Aunt Martha were sitting. He looked up toward the doctor, then down at his hands, raising them before his face and trying to see them. "It's dark in here. — Put up the shades. Turn on the light! I can't see!"

He struck out with his fists, hitting as if the dark were something he could fight. Then he clawed at it, trying to tear a hole in the darkness so that he could see through, squinting, forcing himself to see. He was gasping for breath like a spent runner, his arms thrashing the air. Jimmy's mother sat stunned, staring wide-eyed at her son. She started to rise, but her legs would not bear her weight. Aunt Martha and Miss Moore came to her, helping her to the half-crazed boy. She sank to her knees beside him. Jimmy's arms were still waving wildly, his clenched fists fighting the darkness. One fist struck her in the face.

"Jimmy, this is mother." The pain in her voice seemed to reach him, and he realized he had struck his mother.

"Mom," he whimpered, and again, "Mom." He turned his empty face toward her. She gathered him in her arms.

His tense muscles slowly relaxed.

The nurse handed Mrs. Carter a pill that would help Jimmy go to sleep. "Here, son," his mother said softly. "See if you can swallow this." Jimmy let her give him the pill, and didn't seem to mind when she spilled part of the water over him.

He was exhausted. His mother held him close, gently rocking him. Then she laid him slowly back upon the pillow, quietly smoothing his forehead above the disfigured eyes. Jimmy slept. Dr. Wallace helped Mrs. Carter to her feet. "I would suggest," he said, carefully controlling the emotion his face showed, "that you get in touch with the State Department of Rehabilitation."

"What's that?" she asked blankly.

"That's where handicapped people receive personal guidance," he told her. "They will supply a welfare worker to teach Jimmy how to get around."

"How can he get around if he's blind?" she asked.

"With a cane or a guide dog," Dr. Wallace explained. "Many blind people lead a very normal life." He turned to Aunt Martha. "Why don't you take your sister home and make her rest? Jimmie will sleep until morning."

"Morning!" Mrs. Carter repeated. "There will be no morning for him."

"Come, Ruth." Aunt Martha took her sister's arm, and the two women walked slowly toward the hospital corridor. Mrs. Carter stopped to look back at the sleeping boy. Shaking her head sadly she said, "Jimmy is entering a long, dark corridor. I wonder where it will lead him. How can he play like the other boys? He was always so active. What will his life be now?"

Chapter
TWO

A FEW DAYS LATER an orderly came in to help Jimmy get dressed. He handed Jimmy his shirt. "Can you put this on, or do you want me to help?"

"Of course I can dress myself." Jimmie took the shirt, but couldn't find the armholes.

"Wait a minute, you've got it upside down." The orderly held the shirt while Jimmy put his arms into the sleeves and buttoned the shirt, but the buttons didn't come out even with the buttonholes.

Jimmy was getting fidgety as he unbuttoned the shirt to start over. "Guess you'll have to dress me," he said weakly.

"You can do it," the orderly said. "Didn't you ever get up early in the morning and dress in the dark? Pretend you've got your eyes shut."

Jimmy stopped. His arms dropped to his sides. "I don't have to pretend," he said.

The orderly buttoned the first button and Jimmy went on from there. Then the orderly handed him his trousers and Jimmy started to put them on.

"Hold on there," the orderly said, "let's start over. You've got your right foot into the left trouser leg."

Jimmy finally got the trousers on, and then his socks. Fortunately, socks have no right or left; but when it came to his shoes, he had to be told which was which. He put them on and the orderly tied the lacings for him.

Miss Moore came in. "How would you like to go down to the sun parlor, Jimmy?" she asked cheerfully.

"How can I go anywhere?" Jimmy sounded very helpless.

"You can walk." She took his arm. "Now stand up."

Jimmy stood up slowly, holding the bedpost very tightly with one hand.

"Turn the bed loose. You're not taking it with you." Miss Moore's voice was kind but firm.

"I can't go." Jimmy shrank back.

"Come on," she urged. "There's nothing wrong with your feet. Just take one step."

He took one step and stopped. "I don't know what I'm stepping on."

"You're stepping on the floor," Miss Moore said quietly. "Now take another step. I'll help you."

"Let me alone," Jimmie protested. "You can see. You don't know what it's like. There's just nothing around me. I can't walk on nothing. Everything's empty. Take me back."

"Slide your foot forward," she encouraged, "then reach out with your other foot. The floor will be there."

Jimmy walked as if he were on roller skates, but at last reached the sun parlor. He was sitting there when his mother came to tell him of her visit to the State Department of Rehabilitation. "I met a Miss Thompson who promised to help you," she said.

"Help me do what?" Jimmy asked.

"Why, anything you want to do."

"Can she help me go Scouting? She can't help me do nothin'." Jimmy kicked the leg of his chair.

"She's anxious to meet you, Jimmy. I told her you were captain of your baseball team and that you were taking part in —"

"Yeah, *was* captain," Jimmy cut in. "I couldn't even get out to the lot now — after what Mike Adams did to me."

"You know he didn't do it on purpose."

"That doesn't help me to see. I told him not to do it."

"His mother came over to see me, Jimmy. The boys won't let Mike play with them."

"Serves him right."

Mrs. Carter changed the subject. "Miss Thompson said you might try to get a guide dog."

"Dog? What's the good of a dog now? How could we play?"

"This isn't just a dog. It's a *guide* dog. They are trained to lead people who can't see," his mother explained. "Miss Thompson will tell you all about them."

Miss Moore interrupted to take Jimmy back to bed, but he did not sleep well that night. He dreamed that he was running after a dog; but as soon as he got near it, the dog took off through the air like a plane, and he followed it, running on nothing, with nothing all around him.

He reached for the dog, and as it turned to look at him he saw that it was Mike. Jimmy called, "Don't do it!" Suddenly Mike disappeared in a blinding flash of light

with a noise like a great crash of thunder, and Jimmy was
falling — falling with nothing to hold on to — and he
screamed in terror.

Then one of the nurses was with him, her hand on his
arm. "What's the matter, Jimmy?"

He grabbed for her hand. "Catch me!" he cried. "Hold
me!"

She took him into her arms. "You've been having a
nightmare, young man."

Gradually the dream faded, and he was back in the
hospital with the nurse giving him a soothing drink. She
sat beside him until he went peacefully to sleep.

When his mother and Aunt Martha came to take
Jimmy home the next day, they brought him an ice-
cream cone. While he was eating it, Aunt Martha came
over to him.

"Jimmy," she said. "I want you to try these on and
see how they look."

"Don't, Martha, not now," Mrs. Carter said.

"One time is as good as another," Aunt Martha answered. "Hold still, Jimmy." She put a pair of glasses on
him, hooking the metal loops behind his ears.

"What's that for?" Jimmy asked.

"Just a pair of glasses," his mother said quietly.

"Glasses, for me?"

"Your eyes are not quite healed, Jimmy," Aunt Martha
explained. "They don't need to be bandaged, but these
glasses will help keep out the dust."

"I bet they're dark glasses! I bet you want to hide my
eyes. You mean they're ugly!" The ice-cream cone fell
unnoticed to the floor. "Here, take 'em, I don't want 'em!"

He snatched off the glasses. "I don't need 'em! How can I go anywhere, ever? How can I do anything but just sit?"

His mother came over and put her arms around him. "We don't know, Jimmy. This is not going to be easy for any of us."

She sank into a chair with her arms still around him, drawing him into her lap as if he were five instead of eleven. And as if he were five, Jimmy dropped his head upon her shoulder and cried.

Jimmy went home in a taxi sitting between his mother and Aunt Martha. They got out of the cab in front of the house; the driver half carried, half led Jimmy up the walk to the front door.

Carolyn, his nine-year-old sister, was watching for them through the window. She opened the door and stood there awkwardly, not knowing what to do. As the cab driver turned away, Jimmy started to take a step and his toe bumped the threshold. Carolyn jumped forward and caught him as he stumbled, hugging him. "Here, Jimmy, let me help you."

That was all it took to restore Jimmy's self-confidence. "Out of the way, Midget. Who's helping who?"

Then his mother took him firmly by the arm and led him to his room. She helped him take off his shoes and jacket, and Jimmy lay down on his bed. The trip had been quite a strain, and he was tired.

That afternoon Carolyn came quietly to his door. "Jimmy!" she said softly. "Are you awake?"

"Yeah, Midget. What do you want?"

"Chuck and Art are here," she told him. "Do you want

to see them — I mean, do you want them to come in?"

"Aw, they don't want to see me." He sounded defiant.

"But that's what they came for," Carolyn said.

"Then why didn't they come to the hospital?"

"Same reason I didn't. We weren't allowed."

"Oh! I never thought of that." Jimmy hesitated. It was lonesome in his room. "Okay, Midget," he said. "Tell 'em to come on in."

Jimmy heard their footsteps as they came down the hall and stopped at his door.

"Hi," the two boys said as they came in slowly and stood just inside the door.

Jimmy turned to look in the direction of their voices as if trying to see them. "Hi," he answered.

Chuck made a half-hearted gesture of greeting with his hand, but stopped as he realized that Jimmy could not see him. He and Art looked at each other. They didn't know how to behave around a blind person.

Chuck went to the chair beside Jimmy's bed and sat very straight. Art tiptoed quietly to a chair at the table that Jimmy used for a desk. There was an embarrassed silence. Neither of them could think of anything to say.

"Where are you fellows?" Jimmy asked.

"Here," they answered in chorus.

"Oh!" Jimmy did not know exactly where "here" was.

Art picked up one of Jimmy's books, thumbed through it, and turned toward Jimmy to make some remark about it. Jimmy's eyes, seared by the firecracker, stopped him and he decided to say nothing about the book.

"Is there anything I can get you, Jimmy?" Chuck asked. "Glass of water or something?"

"No thanks," said Jimmy, and the conversation died again.

Carolyn came in with three glasses of lemonade and a plate of cookies on a tray. She stopped in the doorway, a feeling of shyness coming over her also.

"Hey, lemonade!" Chuck said.

She gave him a glass, offered him the cookies, and went over to serve Art. Then she stood beside Jimmy's bed, wondering what to do. "Jimmy," she said timidly, "here's your lemonade."

Jimmy thought of the bent glass tube he had used in the hospital and the way the nurses had helped him. He couldn't let Carolyn help him; she was his kid sister. He was older and always had been the boss.

He swung his feet over the edge of the bed and came up to a sitting position, reaching for the glass as Carolyn extended it. Their hands almost collided. Carolyn quickly drew back, then reached forward and put the glass into his outstretched hand.

Jimmy took it clumsily, spilling a few drops, but no one noticed. As he started to bring the glass to his lips, he tilted it a little sideways, almost spilling it again.

Carolyn came to the rescue. "Wait a minute, Jimmy, I guess I filled it too full." She steadied the glass to an upright position, guiding it as he brought it to his lips.

"Hey, that's good," Jimmy said, meaning both the lemonade and his achievement in drinking it. "What about those cookies?" he added.

Again came the awkward situation of Carolyn's getting the plate under his extended hand. Jimmy knocked a cookie off the plate as he picked up one next to it, but no one said anything, and Carolyn, looking at the two boys in turn, stooped to pick up the cookie and slipped it into her apron pocket. She put the plate of cookies on the desk beside Art and left the room.

"How about another cookie, Midget?" Jimmy ordered.

"Oh, she's gone out," said Art. "I'll bring them to you."

"Never mind, just hand me one," Jimmy said, and saved that situation.

The food seemed to remove the tension. It was so much easier to talk while drinking and eating. Jimmy wanted to be brought up to date on what had happened on the playground and in the Boy Scout troop.

"Mike Adams hasn't been coming to the Scout meetings," Art began.

"It's a good thing," said Jimmy. "He'd better not come around me, either."

"He's changed," Chuck said. "Seems like he's gotten sorta mean. He didn't used to be."

"The fellows don't have much to do with him," Art went on, reaching for another cookie.

"And I don't want to talk about him," Jimmy told them. "I don't want to see him, ever!" he added with a bitter note in his voice.

"But, Jimmy, you'll run into him at school and places," Art reminded him.

"Golly, how are you going to get to school?" Chuck asked, taking Jimmy's empty glass and putting it on the desk.

"Yeah, how?" Jimmy was trying to hide his feelings. "Mom was talking to some woman about getting me a guide dog. Sounds silly."

"Hey, I've read about those dogs," said Chuck. "They lead people swell. Kids in the 4-H Clubs raise 'em."

"How do you mean, raise 'em?" Art asked. "Like a project?"

"The schools where they train the dogs lend the puppies to the 4-H kids," Chuck explained.

"Just lend 'em?" Art wanted to know.

"Yeah. The kids raise 'em until the dogs are old enough to train," said Chuck. "Then they give 'em back to the school."

"That sounds like fun," said Art. "What kind of schools are they, Chuck?"

"Oh, just schools where they teach the dogs to lead people."

"A dogs' school?" Art asked.

"I think they teach the people how to walk with the dogs, too," Chuck told him.

Jimmy had been listening. "Guess I'll find out all about it when that woman talks to me," he said, "but it won't do any good. I can't walk around with just a dog."

"I'll bet you can," Chuck argued. "Those dogs are awful smart. They've got movies about 'em."

"I don't know." Jimmy was noncommittal. "I'd like to have a dog. It's gonna get kind of lonesome not being able to go anywhere or do anything."

"You can do things," Chuck told him, trying to convince himself at the same time.

"Yeah? What?" Jimmy asked.

"I don't know. Wait till the guide-dog woman tells you." Chuck also was wondering.

Chapter
THREE

Jᴵᴹᴹʏ, this is Miss Thompson," said Mrs. Carter, standing in the doorway to his room.

"Good morning, Jimmy." Hearing Miss Thompson's cheerful voice, Jimmy sat up and swung his feet over the side of the bed.

"Good morning, Miss Thompson. I've been waiting for you."

"That's fine." Miss Thompson drew up a chair to sit opposite him.

"Mom's been telling me so much that I don't know when she's kidding."

"I'll leave you to get acquainted." Mrs. Carter turned to go. "Call me if you want anything."

"Thank you," Miss Thompson said. "Now, Jimmy. What's all this about kidding?"

"That's what I want to know. Am I really getting a dog, and will it take me where I want to go? How am I going to play with the other fellows or go on Scout hikes? And hey, what about going to school?"

"Wait a minute!" Miss Thompson laughed. "One at a time. I didn't promise to get a guide dog. I said we'd try to get one."

"But how can a dog know where I want to go?" Jimmy asked.

"You will learn how to direct it, and I know you will love it, Jimmy."

"Sure, I'd like a dog. But how will I get it, and can it take me to school?"

"I'll talk to your mother about the dog, and as for going to school, you will have to learn Braille first."

"What's Braille?" Jimmy asked.

"It's the language of the blind."

"But why can't I talk English?"

Miss Thompson laughed. "You will talk English, but read and write in Braille."

"Heck, what's the good of that if I can't go places and do things?"

"You can go anywhere you want to go and do almost anything you want to do," she said.

"But I can't see!" Jimmy protested.

"I realize you are blind. So are about three hundred thousand other people in the United States. Some of them are college professors, musicians, lawyers, and businessmen," Miss Thompson told him. "I know a high-school student who is a radio ham. He built and is operating his own amateur short-wave station."

"And he can't see?"

"No. He is totally blind, just as you are, but he didn't give up and quit trying. Look, Jimmy, a person who is blind is just the same as anyone else with his eyes closed."

"How do you mean? I don't get it." He was puzzled.

"When people talk over the telephone, they can't see

each other," she explained. "And over the radio everyone sees with his ears."

"But seeing with my ears won't help me go places by myself, and you know it." Jimmy's voice trembled in spite of himself.

"But you will, Jimmy," Miss Thompson encouraged. "That's what I will teach you. You will see with your mind and memory. You can find your way around this room, can't you?"

"I don't know. I guess so — but that's not going places."

"Let's try. Describe your furniture and tell me where it is located," Miss Thompson instructed.

"My desk is over there," Jimmy began, pointing, "but I don't remember if the chair is in front of it or on the side."

"That's what I mean," she told him. "Come, we'll stand in the doorway and get a mental picture of your room."

As Jimmy started for the door, she stopped him. "Wait a minute, your closet door is open just enough to give you a bad bump."

Jimmy drew back sharply. "That's what I'm telling you, Miss Thompson. I'd bump into everything."

"Not if you hold your arms properly. Let your right arm hang in front of you with the palm out, and put your left arm across your chest." She demonstrated with Jimmy's arms.

"You mean I'm to walk like this?"

"Yes. Your left arm across your body will protect you like the bumber of an automobile, and your right hand will feel things like the antenna on an insect."

"Insect!" Jimmy exclaimed. "You mean the antenna for a television set."

"It's the same thing," she said. "The feeler on an insect is called an antenna, and we borrowed the word for radio and television."

"So I'm an insect now." Jimmy waved his right arm. "I've got a bumper like an automobile and an antenna like an insect."

"You walk this way in the house," Miss Thompson explained. "There is a different method for out of doors."

"I still say I can't do it," he argued. "How will I know which way I'm going?"

"We use the face of the clock for directions," she said. "Like they do on a fighter bomber. The gunner knows just where to look when he is told an enemy plane is coming in at two o'clock or five o'clock. You are always in the center of the clock. In front of you is twelve o'clock, behind you is six, three is to your right, and nine is on your left."

"Hey, I'm a jet bomber," Jimmy exclaimed. "Navigator to turret gunner, telephone post coming in at eleven o'clock. Wham!"

"If you can teach that method to your friends and the Boy Scout troop," she told him, "it will keep them from saying, 'It's over this way' or 'down that way.'"

"Say, this is getting to be interesting," Jimmy admitted.

Miss Thompson hugged him. "We haven't even started, but that's enough for this time. Practice walking around the house the way I showed you, and tomorrow I will bring the first piece of equipment for your new way of life."

"Now what?" Jimmy asked.

"It's a white cane," she answered.

"A white cane! I'm an insect, an automobile, a clock, and now I'm a drum major. Okay, what else?"

"But you don't use it like a drum major, Jimmy. Only blind people are permitted to carry white canes. It will be a great help and protection for you."

"What is it, a club?" Jimmy was curious.

"We'll learn about that tomorrow," she told him. "Now get busy and memorize everything you can about your room and the house."

"Yeah. If I can remember it all."

"Sighted people look at many things without really seeing them, but you will become observant," she said.

"Oh boy!" Jimmy said. "I'll be like Sherlock Holmes. I'll see things the rest of the gang never notice."

"You're right." Miss Thompson rose from her chair. "I think you've had an excellent lesson. Now I'll talk with your mother about an application for a guide dog."

"Gee, tell 'em to hurry up!"

"Don't be impatient, Jimmy. It may take several weeks or even months. See you tomorrow. Good-by."

"Good-by, Miss Thompson." Jimmy started studying the things in his room and called Carolyn to help him. "Hey, Midget! Come here a minute."

She came and stood quietly in the doorway.

Jimmy waited a few moments and then called again, "Hey, Carolyn! Where are you?"

"Right here," she answered.

"Oh!" Jimmy was startled. He expected her to answer from somewhere else in the house, but she was standing right next to him. "You scared me."

"You called, didn't you?" she asked. "What's wrong with you, Jimmy?"

"I don't know. Seemed like you jumped out at me and said 'Boo.' I didn't know you were here."

Carolyn looked at him thoughtfully. "Maybe I should have said something when I came to the door."

"Yeah," Jimmy agreed. "How else would I know?"

"Well, now you know I'm here, what did you call me for?"

"Oh, I almost forgot. I've got to study the arrangement of my room."

"That's silly," Carolyn objected. "You've lived here most of your life. You know what it's like."

"Oh yeah?" Jimmy said. "That's what you think!"

"You mean you don't know where things are?" she asked.

"All right, Miss Smarty, you know this room. Suppose you tell me with your eyes shut," he said. "Come here, I'll hold my hands over your eyes. Now, where's my chest of drawers?"

"Over there." Carolyn pointed.

"Where is 'there'?" Jimmy asked.

"What do you mean?"

"Can you tell time?"

"What's that got to do with it?" Carolyn asked. "Of course I can."

"Well then, what o'clock is my chest of drawers?"

Carolyn reached up and took his hands from her face. "You feel all right, Jimmy?" She looked at him steadily. "You're sure talking funny."

"I've got to learn directions by the face of the clock. You and Mom have to help me."

"You know I want to help you, Jimmy."

"I've got to remember exactly where everything is. Tell me if I'm right."

"Okay, I'm ready," Carolyn said.

"On my desk at the left-hand corner are some books," he began. "Now let's see, there's *Tom Sawyer, Treasure Island*, and — but wait, tell me what order they are in. I'll have to know them by their shape or size or something."

"But Jimmy." Her voice was soft. "You won't be reading them."

Jimmy stopped. "Oh!" he said slowly. "That's right." And all the fun went out of the game.

The next morning Miss Thompson brought Jimmy his white cane and showed him how to use it.

"Hold the cane so that the point touches the ground in front of you," she said. "That will show you where it is safe to walk."

Jimmy practiced walking across the room several times. "Now let's try it outdoors." Miss Thompson led the way. Jimmy closed the front door. "This is like playing blind man's buff, Miss Thompson."

"Yes," she smiled, "only you you must try not to catch anything."

Jimmy took a few steps across the porch and stopped. "How far am I from the edge?" He reached out with his cane.

"Wait. I'll start you from the edge of the porch," Miss Thompson said. "Now count your steps back to the door. Then you will know how many steps to take."

Jimmy started to count as he walked. He was so busy counting that he paid no attention to his white cane. Suddenly there was a thud. "Ouch!" he cried.

"Watch out, Jimmy!" Miss Thompson called, too late. "Did you hurt yourself?"

"Guess I wasn't looking." Jimmy rubbed his head. "Anyway, I found the door."

"I didn't tell you to find it with your head, Jimmy," she said.

Jimmy turned around. "The bump made me forget my count."

"We'll try it again. This time hold your cane the way I showed you," she advised.

Jimmy carefully counted his steps to the door, turned around, and started on the big adventure. He stopped in front of Miss Thompson. "I know where you are," he said.

"That's fine. How do you know?"

"You're wearing perfume." Jimmy grinned. "And anyhow, I just seem to feel that there is something in front of me."

"That's what we call facial vision," she explained.

"What's that?" he asked.

"That is seeing with your face, sometimes called the third eye. I will help you develop it."

"You mean because I'm blind I'll get another eye?"

"No, Jimmy. Everyone has that sense, but we'll talk about it later. Now let's get started."

"Okay. I ought to be at the end of the porch," Jimmy said.

"You are. Reach down with your cane, find the top step, then put your foot on it."

Jimmy hesitated. "There's nothing to hold on to. I might fall."

"You don't need anything to hold on to. I'll steady you for the first step; then you can go on alone," she encouraged him.

He was trembling, his muscles tense, and his feet seemed glued to the porch. He slid one foot forward and stepped out into space. Slowly he lowered his foot, and the top step seemed to come up to meet him. Haltingly he worked his way down the steps.

When they reached the sidewalk, they turned to the left.

"Hold your cane in your left hand and walk as I have shown you," Miss Thompson instructed.

Jimmy took a step forward. He remembered the little low wall at the edge of the lawn and swung his cane to the left to feel for it.

"That's it," she encouraged. "Every few steps you can do that."

"I wanted to see if I was going in a straight line," Jimmy explained.

He walked on slowly, occasionally touching the wall with his cane. He had just taken a few steps when the sound of a truck roared toward him. Jimmy stiffened and drew his shoulders in tightly, close to his body. He couldn't move; he just stood and waited for the truck to hit him.

"What's the matter, Jimmy?" Miss Thompson came close so he could sense her presence, then gently laid her hand on his arm.

"That — that truck!" Then Jimmy slowly relaxed as

he heard the truck pass him and go rattling up the street.
"I thought it was going to hit me."

"But you're on the sidewalk, Jimmy. You're safe here."

"I don't know, Miss Thompson. It's scary."

"Well, I'm with you and I'll watch out for things. Let's go on with our lesson."

Jimmy moved slowly until he came to the end of the wall and then stopped.

"What have you found?" she asked.

"This ought to be the driveway. The wall ends here."

"You're right," she told him.

Jimmy walked on until he came to the other side of the driveway. "This must be the Whitneys' front yard. It feels like grass."

Slats Anderson, who had been watching Jimmy from across the street, came over to join them. "Hi, Jimmy. Learning to walk?"

"It's Slats, isn't it?" Jimmy asked.

"Yeah. How'd you know?"

"Recognized your voice," Jimmy told him.

"I've been watching you," said Slats.

"I'm learning to walk with my eyes closed," Jimmy said. "Think you could do it?"

"Sure, that's easy." Slats boasted. "You're just walking down the sidewalk."

"All right," Miss Thompson suggested. "Give me your handkerchief and let me blindfold you. Then we'll try it."

Slats wasn't sure he liked that, but he couldn't very well back out. Blindfolded, he started swaggering down the street. He took two or three steps, then stopped.

"Go on, Slats," Miss Thompson encouraged, "it's easy."

Slats started forward and stepped on the lawn at his side. Angrily he snatched off the handkerchief. "I don't have to do this," he said.

"No," Miss Thompson agreed, "but Jimmy does, and he needs the help of all of his friends."

Slats looked at Jimmy, feeling just a little ashamed of having teased him. "Sure," he said, "I'll help. What do you want me to do?"

"Nothing special. Just be a good Scout." Turning to Jimmy she said, "I think that will be enough for today. Now you can find your way back."

"This is hard work," Jimmy complained. "I feel like I've played a double-header. Will you lead me home?"

"I'll lead him back," Slats volunteered.

"Jimmy's through with being led," Miss Thompson told them. "Now Jimmy, put your cane in your right hand and go back the way you came."

Jimmy started. When he got to the low wall, he stopped to rest a few minutes. "This is awful slow, Miss Thompson. It would take me a year to get anywhere."

"You'll go quicker with practice," she answered, "but if you get a guide dog, you won't worry about going slowly."

"Hey, you gonna get one of those blind-eye dogs?" Slats asked.

"They're called guide dogs," Jimmy corrected Slats. "Not blind-eye dogs." He started walking again and heaved a big sigh when he came to the gate. "This ought to be home," he said. Slats looked at Jimmy with secret admiration. "So long, Jimmy. Good luck!"

"Thanks, Slats. So long."

Slats stood and watched as Jimmy walked up the steps holding the cane in front of him, then crossed the porch and found the front door, this time with his cane.

"The knob is on your left," Miss Thompson said.

"Is the knob always on the left?" Jimmy asked.

"No, of course not. It isn't that easy," she said laughing. "You know yourself that if the knob is on the left of the *outside* of the door, it's got to be on the right of the *inside*."

"Sure thing!" Jimmy agreed. He opened the door, to be snatched at once into his mother's arms. "Oh, I'm so glad you're back! My poor boy!"

"But he isn't a poor boy," Miss Thompson protested. "He got along beautifully."

"You're right," Mrs. Carter admitted. "Carolyn and I were watching. Jimmy, I'm proud of you."

Jimmy straightened his shoulders, and somehow he didn't feel so tired.

"What can I do to help him, Miss Thompson?" Carolyn asked.

"Jimmy must learn to get along by himself," Miss Thompson said. "You'll have to take a few bumps, Jimmy. It won't hurt you."

"It sure won't feel *good*," Jimmy protested.

"How did it feel to walk alone like a man?" Miss Thompson asked.

"Okay," Jimmy answered, and added under his breath, "if you call *that* walking like a man."

"How soon can he try this again?" his mother asked.

"I'll come back tomorrow," Miss Thompson said. "You'll get along even better then, Jimmy."

"Yeah," he mumbled. "We'll go on a Scout hike tomorrow, huh?" And Jimmy felt tired all over again.

"Will he ever walk well enough to do that?" his mother asked.

"That will depend upon Jimmy," Miss Thompson answered.

"Sure he can do it!" Carolyn said. She walked over and put her hand on Jimmy's arm.

"Thanks, Midget." Jimmy wished he were as sure as Carolyn.

Chapter

FOUR

Carolyn," Jimmy called, "can you come here?" He had been home from the hospital for several weeks, and his mother was at work.

"Just a minute," Carolyn answered. She was in the kitchen mopping the floor. This had been Jimmy's chore before he lost his sight, and he did not know that Caroyln had taken it over. She set the mop upright in the pail and went quickly to Jimmy's room.

"All right," she said as she approached his door. Then as he stood in the open doorway she continued quietly, "What is it, Jimmy?"

"Look, Midget." Jimmy was serious. "You know I never minded you borrowing my things, but now you'll have to tell me about it."

"Tell you about what? I haven't borrowed anything."

"You borrowed my blue sweater again, and you didn't put it back."

"I didn't take it," she protested.

"I left it on this coat hanger," Jimmy argued, "and now it's gone."

"Let me look." Carolyn went to the closet. "Here it is on the floor in the corner."

35

"Oh, I'm sorry, Midget," Jimmy apologized, and added, "Thank you," as she handed the sweater to him.

"It's all right," she said. "Now if you'll get out of here I'll straighten up your room."

Jimmy went to the kitchen for a glass of water. Holding his hands as Miss Thompson had shown him, he walked briskly toward the sink. Suddenly there was a crash — clatter — bang!

Carolyn heard the noise and rushed to the kitchen. She saw a stream of water flowing over her clean floor and spreading fanwise as it traveled. Jimmy was lying on the floor, wrestling with the mop, one foot in the overturned pail. It looked as though he were trying to swim in the shallow soapy water.

Carolyn didn't want to laugh, but she couldn't help a giggle as she tried to ask, "Are you hurt, Jimmy?" But all he got was her gurgle of laughter.

"What is all this?" Jimmy was angry.

"Wait, I'll help you up!" Carolyn pulled at his arm, but was laughing so hard that she had no strength. She tugged again and her feet slipped in the soapy water. She splashed down beside him.

It had all happened so quickly that Jimmy didn't know just where he was. He tried to raise himself on his hands, but they slipped on the wet waxed floor and he splashed back into the water. That set Carolyn laughing all over again.

Finally Jimmy got his foot out of the pail and Carolyn scrambled back to her feet to help Jimmy up.

"What happened?" Jimmy asked.

"Well, if you must know," she told him, "I've been

mopping the floor for Mother since your accident. I just finished when you called me."

"Oh!" Jimmy was getting the picture. "You left the mop and pail in the middle of the floor."

"I just left them for a minute."

"And I fell over them."

"And you messed up my clean floor," Carolyn complained.

"I'm sorry, Midget. I messed me up, too."

"It's all right, I can mop it up again. But you did look funny."

"Now I'll have to take a bath and change my clothes," Jimmy grumbled.

"I guess it was my fault," Carolyn said, "but I didn't know you were coming to the kitchen."

"You're all wet too, aren't you?" Jimmy asked. "I heard you fall."

"Sure. I'd love to have a movie of us." Carolyn laughed again.

Jimmy had just finished dressing, with his hair wet and plastered down, when the doorbell rang.

He opened the door for Miss Thompson. "Good morning, Jimmy," she greeted him. "My, we look all spruced up."

"Yes," Jimmy answered. "I — I had an accident."

"What happened?" Miss Thompson asked as she entered.

"I was holding my hands the way you showed me," Jimmy complained, "but I fell over a pail of water Carolyn left in the kitchen."

"That is something of a problem," she said. "You must see with your feet also when you are indoors."

"I would have found it with my cane, but you won't let me use it in the house."

"This sort of thing doesn't happen often, Jimmy. A cane is awkward indoors around furniture, even though you have learned to handle it so well on the street."

"Where will we go today?" Jimmy asked. "We've been all around this block, and I think I know it."

"We're going to do something different today," she said. "Let's go to the dining room. We'll need the table for our first lesson in Braille."

"Oh yes! You told me I'd have to learn Braille to get my guide dog."

"No. You'll have to learn it to go to school."

"I was studying the Morse code in the Scouts," Jimmy said. "Why can't I use that?"

"You can use that for telegraphy," she answered, "but you read and write in Braille." She sat beside him at the table and opened a Braille primer.

"Before I let you feel the Braille dots, I want you to get an idea of what it is," Miss Thompson went on. "We use only six dots in the entire Braille language."

"To make all the letters?" Jimmy asked.

"Yes. The alphabet, the numbers, and the punctuation marks are all made by different arrangements of the six dots," she explained. "We start with a 'cell,' arranged like the six dots on dice or a domino. Two vertical rows of three dots each."

Cell

1 ● ● 4
2 ● ● 5
3 ● ● 6

"Okay," said Jimmy. "I can see that."

"Each dot has a name, or rather a number. Starting at the left, the top dot is number one, then reading down the second dot is number two, and the bottom dot is number three. The three dots on the right, starting at the top, are four, five, and six."

"I think I've got it," Jimmy said. "You just count down on the left, one, two, three, and down on the right, four five, and six. That's easy."

"Braille is easy," she agreed. "See if you can feel this one raised dot."

Jimmy felt over the paper a while and discovered a little point like a typewriter period.

"I've found something," he said, "but this can't be it— it's too small."

"But it is," she told him. "That's A, the first letter of the alphabet. Now feel this." She laid his finger gently on another spot in the paper. "This is the letter B, made up of dots one and two. Can you feel them?"

"It just feels like a longer dot," Jimmy complained.

"Yes, but it is two dots, like a colon. Now feel this one. This is the letter C, dots one and four. Do you remember where they are?"

"I think it's the two top dots, isn't it?"

"That's right," she said. "The first ten letters of the Braille alphabet are made by the arrangement of the four top dots, numbers one, two, four, and five, like this:

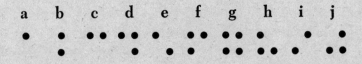

"The next ten letters of the alphabet are a repetition of the first ten with the addition of dot number three. So by adding dot number three to A, it becomes K, B becomes L, and so on.

k   l   m   n   o   p   q   r   s   t

"The rest of the alphabet follows this pattern by the addition of dot six; then K becomes U, L becomes V. The French language, where Braille originated, does not use W, so the letter W is the exception and is a reverse R."

u   v   w   x   y   z

"Is Braille written in French?" Jimmy asked.

"The French people write it in French, but we write it in English," Miss Thompson said. "It was created by Louis Braille, who was born in France, in 1809."

"Oh, it's named after him. Was he blind?"

"Yes, Jimmy, he became blind. He was the son of a harnessmaker, and while he was playing in his father's shop one day, when he was a very small boy, Louis accidentally stuck a sharp pointed awl into his eye."

"In both of his eyes?" Jimmy asked.

"No, but both eyes became affected," she went on.

"After he was blind, he made up a code for himself by punching holes in bits of scrap leather from his father's shop."

"A secret code?"

"Well, it wasn't secret, but no one else could read it."

"Hey, that gives me an idea!" Jimmy said. "What was his code like?"

"I just told you. He punched holes in bits of leather, but it wasn't long before he ran out of scraps. Then he found that, by punching holes partway through, he made a dent on one side of the leather and a bump on the other. He also found it was easier to feel the bumps than the dents, and that by hammering down the bumps he could use the same piece of leather many times. That's the way the Braille system started."

"And he thought all this out when he was just a little boy?" Jimmy asked.

"Oh no!" she explained. "The Braille system has been changed, improved, and simplified many times until it arrived at its present form. And you may be interested to know, Jimmy, that this same Braille cell is used by the blind all over the world. It's a sort of universal language."

"I'll bet you can't write Chinese in Braille," Jimmy said.

"You'd lose your bet," Miss Thompson told him. "The Chinese don't spell out the words as we do, but they have symbols and signs in Braille that make Chinese words. I told you it was international, but we'll be satisfied just to study it in English. Now let's get back to our lesson."

Jimmy's unaccustomed fingers found dots where there were none and failed to find dots where they should be. He dropped his hands into his lap. "I'm sorry, Miss

Thompson, I can't see them. They just feel like rough places on the paper."

"You're doing fine, Jimmy," she encouraged. "Don't be impatient."

"I can't do it! It's easy enough for you. You can see and I can't," Jimmy complained.

"But you can see." Miss Thompson corrected him. "You've only lost two eyes."

"Trying to be funny?" he asked. "I only had two eyes."

"You're mistaken, Jimmy," she explained patiently. "You have an eye on the tip of each finger, one at the end of your white cane, one more on the point of each shoe, and the one great eye in the center of your brain. People don't see with their eyes; they see with their brains. They don't feel with their fingers or hear with their ears. When you touch something with your hand, or when you hear a sound, the brain tells you what it is. We're like beetles with a lot of feelers, and you only lost two of yours."

"I think I've lost the feeler that reads Braille," he said.

Carolyn came to the door to ask quietly, "May I interrupt, please?"

"Sure." Jimmy was thankful for the interruption.

"What is it, Carolyn?" Miss Thompson asked.

"Mother made some sandwiches before she left this morning. Will you have lunch with us, Miss Thompson? There's plenty."

Miss Thompson glanced at her wrist watch. "Thank you, Carolyn. I'd like a glass of milk."

Carolyn brought the tray and set it on the dining-room table. When Jimmy reached for the milk, Miss Thompson quietly pushed the Braille primer out of the way.

"What are all those funny little bumps in the pages?" Carolyn asked.

Miss Thompson explained the dots. "You must have Jimmy teach you to read them."

Jimmy began to feel a little important.

"You can leave notes for each other, and it would help Jimmy a great deal if you would study it." Miss Thompson gave Carolyn a card of the Braille alphabet with the regular alphabet printed under each Braille letter.

The sandwiches looked good, and at Carolyn's insistence Miss Thompson joined the children with their lunch while she explained to Carolyn much that she had told Jimmy.

"Of course you can see the raised dots, Carolyn," she said, "and with the alphabet printed under the dots it will be easy for you."

Carolyn drew the primer toward her. "But the alphabet isn't printed in the book."

"You can learn to read the dots without the letters, just as you learn the keys on the piano," Miss Thompson explained.

While they were still eating and talking, the doorbell rang. Carolyn went to the door and called back, "It's Chuck and Art, Jimmy. What shall I tell them?"

"Ask them to come in, Jimmy," Miss Thompson said. "I'd like to meet your friends."

Chuck and Art came in and were very much interested in the sandwiches, so Carolyn had to get two more glasses of milk.

"There's a new boy moved into the neighborhood," Chuck said as Carolyn left the room.

"Yeah?" Jimmy was curious. "Who?"

"His name's Hank Saunders," Art said. "He thinks he can pitch, but he's wild."

"What's he got?" Jimmy asked.

"Got a good curve," Art answered, "if he could find the plate. And we need him."

Jimmy cupped his hand over an imaginary ball, flexed the muscles of his arm.

"He can't take your place," Chuck said, "but since we've lost you and Mike Adams, we've got to have him."

"You wouldn't need him if it weren't for Mike," Jimmy said slowly. He clenched the fist that had been holding the imaginary ball.

"Who is this Mike?" Miss Thompson asked.

Chuck and Art looked at her and then at each other, but did not speak.

"He's the guy who threw the firecracker in my face and did this to me," Jimmy said bitterly.

Miss Thompson looked at Jimmy's face. "We may be able to correct all that, Jimmy." She laid her hand on his shoulder.

"How?" Jimmy challenged. "Can you make me see again?"

"Not with your eyes," she said quietly. "I told you there are many other ways of seeing, and you will learn to use them."

Chapter
FIVE

CAROLYN CAME in with two glasses of milk for the boys, and they all went on eating. Chuck leaned forward, a sandwich in one hand, and picked up the Braille primer. "What's this goofy thing?" he asked between bites.

Again Miss Thompson explained.

"That's not goofy," Jimmy protested. "That's my private secret language."

"Do you sing it or whistle it?" Chuck asked.

"You read it, dumbbell," Jimmy said.

"Here's a Braille alphabet card." Miss Thompson gave a card to each of the boys, "I suggest you learn the alphabet with Jimmy."

Art looked at the little raised dots. "Gee, I'll never learn that!"

"Oh yes you will. It's simple," said Miss Thompson.

"Miss Thompson asked me to teach Carolyn," Jimmy said. "If you fellows learn it, you can write to me while I'm at the guide-dog school."

"When are you gonna get your dog, Jimmy?" Chuck asked.

"Miss Thompson says I've got a lot to learn before I can get it."

"What, for instance?" Art wanted to know.

"Jimmy is starting an entirely new kind of life, and you boys can help him a great deal," Miss Thompson answered.

"Help him? How?" Art and Chuck asked together.

"Just little things. You'll learn them from time to time."

"You mean like Braille?" Chuck fingered the Braille book.

"Yes, that's one, and in trying to see the way Jimmy does."

"I don't know what you mean." Chuck looked at Jimmy's eyes behind the tinted glasses.

"Do you boys know anything about radar?" Miss Thompson asked.

"Hey, is Jimmy gonna get a radar set?" Art leaned across the table toward Jimmy. "Are you, Jimmy?"

"Am I, Miss Thompson?" Jimmy was interested.

"No, Jimmy, but in a way you have one. Each of you has one."

The boys looked blank, and Carolyn moved her chair closer to the circle.

"Do you know what radar is?" Miss Thompson questioned.

"It's what they use to find airplanes," said Chuck.

"It's radio waves that bounce back like an echo, and they catch 'em on a screen," Jimmy put in.

"I know that much," Art said, "but I don't know what it is."

"Then we're all in the same boat." Miss Thompson smiled. "I'm not an electronics engineer, and all I know is that the short radio waves strike an object and bounce back, giving an outline of the object on the screen. We copied that method from the bat."

"You mean the bat that flies?" Jimmy asked.

"Yes. You know the nocturnal bat has very poor sight."

"Is that why they say 'blind as a bat'?" Chuck stopped, clapped his hand over his mouth, and looked at Jimmy.

"That expression is not really accurate," Miss Thompson said. "Bats have eyes but do not use them in flying."

"How do they know that?" asked Art.

"Well, some scientists bandaged a bat's eyes and found it could fly just as well as before; but when they plugged up its ears and left the eyes unbandaged, the bat flew into things."

"That doesn't make sense," Carolyn protested. "It can see with its eyes bandaged and can't see with them open. It sounds funny."

"A bat has very keen hearing and makes a high-pitched, piercing squeak," Miss Thompson explained. "When it flies, the echo of that squeak bounces back to the bat like the radar waves."

"Hey, that's like instrument flying!" Jimmy said.

"Yes," Miss Thompson continued. "That echo shows the bat the sizes and shapes of objects in front of it and how close they are, so that it can fly into the open space around the objects."

"Yeah, but I couldn't do that!" Jimmy complained.

Miss Thompson turned to Jimmy. "Do you remember your first walk with your white cane? When you crossed the porch?"

"I remember I was looking for the front door and found it with my head." Jimmy laughed and the boys joined in with him.

"I mean when you came back and stood in front of me. You said you knew where I was."

"Oh yes," Jimmy said. "You were wearing perfume, and I just knew you were there."

"That was your personal radar," she explained. "You knew I was there without seeing me."

"Could anybody do that?" Chuck asked. "Could I do it?"

"Yes," Miss Thompson said. "We'll call this room a laboratory, and you can watch Jimmy make his scientific experiments. Jimmy, stand here in the middle of the room and clap your hands together once; then tell me what you hear."

Jimmy clapped his hands and said, "I heard somebody clap their hands," and the boys laughed.

"Did you hear it echo from the wall?" Miss Thompson asked.

"No. Let me try it again and I'll listen." Jimmy cocked his head to one side, listening, with his hands apart. Then, as he clapped his hands, Chuck clapped his also and called, "Did you hear the echo, Jimmy?"

"Yeah," Jimmy told him. "I think the echo happened before the sound."

"Another miracle of science," Chuck explained. "The effect preceded the cause."

"All right, scientists." Miss Thompson smiled at them. "Let Jimmy make this experiment."

Jimmy clapped his hands and thought he heard the sound bounce back to him — like radar and like the bat.

"Now I'll lead you to the door." Miss Thompson took his arm. "You can clap your hands again and hear the difference."

Jimmy stood in front of the doorway and clapped his hands. "Why," he said, "it doesn't just sound different, it feels different!"

"Good! You feel the air current," she told him.

"Yes, it's blowing into the room a little."

"That is another way of seeing with your face. You can both hear and feel. Now Jimmy," she went on, "if you will stand close to the wall, I'll let you try something else. Here, stand about two feet from the wall and lean slowly toward it."

"What must I look for?" Jimmy asked.

"I'm going to let you see what you find."

"I found something." Jimmy turned his cheek to the wall. "If I get close enough, it sounds like putting a seashell to my ear."

"That's too close," she said. "Remember you felt the air moving through the door. All the air in this room is moving. It strikes the wall and starts back toward the center of the room, but meets another current of air that stops it."

"Then where does it go?" Jimmy tried to feel the breeze.

"It just piles up against the wall and forms a sort of blanket or cushion," Miss Thompson explained.

"You mean the air is compressed near the wall?" Jimmy asked.

"Yes, Jimmy."

Jimmy turned his face in several directions. "Hey, I think I've got it."

"All right. Now how far are you from the wall?" she asked.

"I think I could reach out my hand and touch it."

"Try it and see," she suggested, and Jimmy found the wall.

"Now step back a few steps and then walk slowly forward," Miss Thompson instructed, "but stop just before you reach the wall and tell me how near you are to it."

The three children watched as Jimmy tried the experiment several times.

"I want you to practice that, Jimmy, until you can walk right up to the wall and stop about one foot from it."

"All right, Miss Thompson, but I wish the walls wore perfume."

She laughed. "Trees and telephone poles also have a blanket of air around them to help you find them."

"Oh, I could find them with my cane," Jimmy said.

"You can find them both ways, and you can tap your cane lightly on the sidewalk to get your radar signal that way."

"Miss Thompson," Chuck asked, "is that why blind people beat the sidewalk with their canes?"

"Yes, Chuck. Some of them hit the sidewalk too often and too hard, and sometimes they do it to attract attention so that people will get out of their way."

"I'm going to practice finding the air waves with my eyes closed," Chuck said. "Or is it only blind people who can do it?"

"Miss Thompson says everybody has it," Jimmy told him. "I'll have to learn it just as you would."

Miss Thompson stood up. "I'll go now and leave you technicians to your laboratory research. You needn't leave your friends, Jimmy. I know my way out."

"Oh, thank you, Miss Thompson. When will I see you again?"

"I'll try to come tomorrow, Jimmy, but you have plenty to work on. You can try these experiments, but don't forget your Braille."

She left the four of them practicing and explaining the process to one another.

Art bumped his head against the wall. "Ouch!" he cried.

"What's the matter, Art?" Jimmy asked. "Did you knock the plaster off?"

"No, I was just trying to find that mattress of air."

"It's just a cushion. Not an inner-spring mattress," Chuck told him.

"I bet it isn't even as thick as a sheet," Art complained.

"Maybe somebody stripped the beds," Jimmy teased.

While they were teasing one another, Carolyn went ahead quietly, finding she could recognize the cushion of air farther and farther from the wall.

That evening, when Jimmy was studying his Braille lesson and paying no attention to what was going on around him, someone walked past him in the living room. It sounded like Carolyn, but it was too heavy for her footsteps; then he thought it might be Carolyn carrying something heavy.

"That you, Midget?" he asked.

"Sure. Who'd you think it was?"

"What are you carrying?" He turned his head toward her.

"Carrying? Nothing. Why?"

"You're walking heavy. It doesn't sound like you."

˙Then he remembered. There had been a quiet air of excitement around the house the last few days. It felt like two or three weeks before Christmas, with whispered conversations between Carolyn and their mother, little conspiracies that left Jimmy on the outside.

He had heard the rattle of paper as packages were quietly unwrapped, and every day his mother, when she came home from work, brought another package which she and Carolyn would whisper about. It had all been very mysterious, but now he understood the mystery, and why Carolyn was walking "heavy."

"Hey," he said. "I'll bet you've got on new shoes. Have you?"

"Why — why, yes," Carolyn answered.

"That's why you sound different," he said. "New school shoes, aren't they, Midget?"

Carolyn hesitated a moment. "Yes," she said slowly.

"And the packages," he went on. "I remember now. I heard Mom and you talking together. School things again, huh?"

Carolyn nodded, but didn't answer.

Jimmy's chin quivered a little, but he gave no other outward sign. "It's all right, Midget. I'm glad you're getting dolled up. Let's see the shoes."

Carolyn held onto the edge of the table and put her foot into his lap.

"They're swell, kid." His fingers went gently over them. "What color are they — black?"

"Yes, they're black and —" She hesitated, then added, "I'm not getting many things, Jimmy."

"Oh, I don't mind. You need new things for school,"

Jimmy said. Carolyn went on to her room to put away her new things and Jimmy sat for a while, his hands lying still upon the Braille book. Finally he closed the book and put it away carefully, so he could find it when he wanted it, went to his own room, and got ready for bed.

Lying in the stillness of his room, he did some thinking. "They tried to be quiet about it all," he said to himself, "so as not to hurt my feelings. Of course I can't go to school. Guess I can't do much of anything."

A feeling of helplessness came over him. He wanted to cry. He was crying inside, but the accident had done something to his tear glands; there were no tears. He just lay there making little sniffling noises and feeling very sorry for himself.

Then he heard footsteps in the hall, the rustle of his mother's skirts as she stopped at his door. He held his breath and lay still. He didn't want her to know. After a few moments he heard her move on toward her own room. He let out his breath in a deep sigh, feeling the darkness of his room close in on him like a fog.

He tried to look through the fog toward his closet. It was over *there* with the door properly closed; and behind that door, neatly arranged on a hanger, was his Scout uniform, the patches showing the merit badges he had earned. He wondered if he would ever earn any new ones, if the door separating him from Scouting would ever open again.

Chapter
SIX

During the days that followed, the household was on its usual schedule, with Carolyn doing the simple chores and Jimmy studying his Braille lessons.

One afternoon Chuck stopped in to tell Jimmy what had happened at the Scout meeting the night before.

"When I get my dog, I can go to Scout meetings with you," Jimmy told him.

"You'll have to teach your dog to collect firewood," Chuck teased.

"Don't you worry," Jimmy boasted. "My dog will have more merit badges than anybody."

"The meeting was keen, Jimmy. Our Scoutmaster, Mr. Douglas, had a man give us a travelogue lecture with colored slides about different birds."

"Yeah?" Jimmy wasn't interested in colored slides.

"He had a tape recorder that gave the bird calls," Chuck went on.

"I would have liked the bird calls." Jimmy cocked his head as if listening. "But the slides wouldn't be any good."

"Mr. Douglas had the fellows imitate the bird calls."

"What birds were they?" Jimmy asked.

"Oh, a lot of them," Chuck said. "I couldn't do the calls, but some of the fellows did. Mike Adams was a whiz."

"Was *he* there?" Jimmy sounded angry.

"Well, yeah." Chuck was sorry he had said anything. "He kinda sat by himself and left early, but he could do bird calls."

"I told you I don't want to talk about him. I don't — Wait a minute." Jimmy sat still, listening.

"What's the matter?" Chuck looked at him sharply.

"Nothing. It's all right, Carolyn went."

"Went where?" Chuck was puzzled.

"To the door, dumb cluck. Didn't you hear the bell?"

"Guess I wasn't noticing," Chuck admitted, then added after a moment, "Carolyn didn't come by here."

"She went through the dining room. Hey, that's Miss Thompson. Come on, Chuck."

"Jimmy!" Carolyn called. "Miss Thompson is here."

"Yeah, I know," Jimmy said as he entered the room. "Hi, Miss Thompson."

"Hello, boys," said Miss Thompson.

"Hi, Miss Thompson," said Chuck. "Jimmy and I were going for a walk."

"I was going to take him around the block," Jimmy told her.

"Oh, that's too easy for you now, Jimmy," she said. "I want you to learn to cross the street."

"Cross the street!" Jimmy echoed. "I don't know about that."

"We'll find out," she answered. "Would you like to go along, Chuck?"

"Sure," said Chuck.

Jimmy didn't like the idea of crossing the street, but got his white cane and walked briskly to the front door, across the porch, down the steps, and to the sidewalk.

"Not so fast," Miss Thompson called.

Jimmy stopped. "Hey, I *was* going fast." He grinned. "I remember my first walk. Gee, I just poked along."

"Which way are we going, Miss Thompson?" asked Chuck.

"We will turn right. There's a signal at the corner."

Chuck watched Jimmy check the landmarks with his cane until they reached the corner.

"Now let's wait here and see if you can hear the signal change," Miss Thompson told Jimmy.

"What must I listen for?" he asked.

"Listen for traffic crossing in front of you. That means the signal is against you; but when it is passing at your side, it's going the same way we are."

Chuck closed his eyes to see if he could tell, then opened them quickly to look.

Jimmy listened intently. "It sounds as if it's going both ways," he said, "or every which way. I don't know."

"You hear a truck with its motor idling behind you on your left; it is staying in one place," Miss Thompson said. "Listen to the car passing in front of you. Hear it?"

Jimmy stepped back quickly. "Miss Thompson, I don't want anything from the other side of the street. I haven't lost anything over there."

"Never mind." Miss Thompson laughed. "We have the signal now. Raise your cane, face straight to the front, and let's go."

Jimmy gripped the cane until his knuckles were white, and stepped off the curb. Little beads of perspiration started on his forehead and ran down into his eyebrows; his white cane swayed gently with the trembling of his whole body. He just walked, not knowing where he was going or how he was getting there. Then he heard the motor of a car at his right elbow and jumped away.

"It's all right, Jimmy," Miss Thompson said, walking beside him. "That car is waiting for a signal."

Jimmy took a few more terrifying steps; then he was across the street.

"That was fine," Miss Thompson told him.

"It's easy at a traffic signal," Chuck put in.

"Oh, yeah?" Jimmy took a deep breath.

"Now listen for the signal again, Jimmy, and we'll start back," Miss Thompson said.

"The signal *is* with us, Miss Thompson," said Chuck.

"Yes, Chuck, but how long has it been with us? We'll lose this signal and start as soon as it is our way again."

"That figures," said Chuck. "We could hurry, but Jimmy couldn't."

"And we shouldn't," Miss Thompson said. "It's better to lose a signal than to lose a leg."

"I think the signal is with us now," Jimmy said, straining to listen and wishing he were safely back home.

"Then let's go. We only have about forty seconds between signals." Miss Thompson stepped off the curb as she spoke.

Jimmy followed her. His feet were moving, but the rest of him seemed paralyzed. He wanted to reach out for her, clutch at something. Terror gripped him as he heard the cars whiz past him. Then he touched the curb and was on the sidewalk again. He felt very weak, very tired.

"Chuck, would you like to lead Jimmy home?" Miss Thompson asked. "He's earned the chance to rest."

"Sure." Chuck reached for Jimmy's hand. "Want me to be a two-legged guide dog?"

Jimmy clutched at Chuck's arm and clung to it. "Take it easy," he panted.

Chuck led him down the street, walking as if Jimmy were made of glass and might break.

"I won't make you work any more today," Miss Thompson told Jimmy when they reached the house. "You can visit with Chuck, but I want you to study your Braille after a while."

"All right, Miss Thompson, but I ought to make Chuck study with me."

"That would be fine," Miss Thompson said.

"Yeah," Chuck said, "only I just remembered I gotta go."

"I'll let you two fight it out." She turned to leave. "Good-by, boys."

" 'By, Miss Thompson," they chorused.

Jimmy turned to Chuck. "You don't have to study if you don't want to."

"I'll have enough studying to do when school starts next week," said Chuck.

"Yeah." Jimmy had a touch of envy in his voice.

On the first day of school, Mrs. Carter got the household up early. Jimmy tried to enter into the cheerful excitement, and for a while felt as if he were part of it.

"Here's your lunch, Carolyn," Mrs. Carter put the box beside Carolyn's plate at the breakfast table.

"Thanks, Mommy." The words came out somewhat muffled by the spoonful of oatmeal going in.

"And be careful," her mother went on. "With books and lunch to carry, you must be extra careful in crossing the street."

Jimmy saw himself crossing the street, his schoolbooks in one hand, his white cane held high in the other, while the cars whizzed past and around him. For the moment he was glad he was not going to school, glad for the protection of staying at home.

"I hate to leave you alone, Jimmy," his mother said, "but you can phone me if anything comes up."

"I'll be all right, Mom. I guess I'll have plenty to do."

"Don't get too busy to eat your lunch," she said. "Carolyn, you must get started. Shouldn't be late the first day."

Carolyn jumped up and Jimmy heard a whirlwind of noise and excitement, ending with a cheerful "Good-by," everybody," just before the front door slammed.

Jimmy heard the rattle of dishes as his mother cleared the table, took them to the kitchen, and stacked them in the sink. Then he heard quick steps going to her room, and a few minutes later she was standing beside him.

"Don't forget, Jimmy, phone me if you want anything." She hugged him to her for a moment, and was gone almost before he could answer.

He sat at the table, seeing the stream of boys and girls coming from all directions and flowing toward the wide doors of the school — some stopping to play in the school grounds, others just running aimlessly around or hurrying inside, or stopping to greet friends whom they had not seen all summer.

He saw his own classroom, and wondered where he would be sitting. Then school was over, and the children poured out of the building, laughing, shouting, racing in all directions, hurrying to the sand lot for a game of baseball. Mike was in the group. Jimmy saw him snatch up a bat and step up to the plate; then Jimmy was pitching and had two strikes on Mike. Mike swung at the third one, and it was Jimmy's bat he was swinging.

Jimmy shook his head to get rid of the picture. "Guess I won't be using my bat and that good old pitcher's glove," he said aloud as if speaking to someone, but no one answered him. The house was quiet — too quiet. He went into his room, turned on the radio, and threw himself across the bed. He didn't listen to the radio; he just let it make a noise and keep him company, but it wasn't much company, so he decided to study his Braille.

He was studying advanced Braille now, in which some words were not completely spelled out. Abbreviations and new characters were used, and all these had to be memorized. Carolyn had helped by holding the book while he recited his lesson, and he needed her to tell him what the new characters meant. Braille was not going very well today. He missed Carolyn more than he wanted to admit.

Jimmy wandered about the house, went back to his room to lie down, then got up to roam around the house again. He was getting hungry, and wished he knew what time it was.

His mother had left some sandwiches in the refrigerator for his lunch, but he didn't know if it was lunchtime. He dialed the time number on the telephone and heard a voice say, "At the tone the time will be eleven-fifteen and thirty seconds."

Jimmy decided to eat his lunch, and went out to the refrigerator to get his sandwiches and drink a glass of milk. That made him feel better. When he went to the sink to rinse out the glass and wash the plate, he found the breakfast dishes where his mother had left them.

"I used to wash the dishes." Jimmy's fingers ran over the pile in the sink. "I bet I can do it now."

He found the dishpan on the nail under the sink and met his first difficulty. The dishes had to be stacked on the drainboard to get the dishpan under the faucets. Jimmy had never realized how many sizes and shapes there were to dishes — plates, bowls, cups and saucers, to be stacked or balanced carefully on top of one another so they would not slip and fall.

Then he searched for the soap powder. Too many things in the kitchen come in paper boxes. Now he was sure he had found it. Jimmy felt the small grains in the box, smelled them, and was not so sure — because there was no odor. He put a pinch in the palm of his hand and moistened it, but it was not slippery, so it could not be soap.

Suddenly he laughed. "Better not tell Mom that I tried to wash the dishes in cornmeal." The box went back on the shelf. Next to it was the soap powder.

It was hard work handling the slippery dishes with his soapy hands and washing them over and over to be sure they were clean. He had to concentrate on everything all

of the time. "It takes an awful lot of dishes for three people to eat breakfast," he complained aloud.

At last he was through. He put away the dishpan, washed out the sink, and cleaned the drainboard. As he wiped the drainboard with a long circular sweep, his hand touched something and he was startled by the crash of china on the floor. His spine stiffened and he caught his breath.

"Oh, gee, gosh — now what have I done?" All his victory turned to defeat. "I hope it wasn't some of Mom's best china." He got the broom and dustpan, wondering what he had broken. Very carefully he fingered the contents of the dustpan and picked up one of the larger pieces; then he sighed with relief.

"I'm glad it was only a saucer. That's not so bad. Mom says there are always more saucers left than cups." He emptied the dustpan into the trash box, wondering what his mother would say when she came home, but he felt proud of his achievement. Victory had returned.

Now he could go back to studying his Braille lesson. Jimmy read the lesson aloud, calling the names of the dots as he felt them: "One, three, five, O; one, three, four, five, N; one, four, C; one, five, E." Then he stopped.

"Hey, I can talk Braille!" he exclaimed. "O-n-c-e, once. I can say it by the numbers of the dots. I've got a secret code like Louis Braille had."

He sat there sending secret code messages to himself, waiting for Art and Chuck to come from school. When they came over that afternoon, Jimmy explained the secret code to them.

"Swell," said Chuck, "but it doesn't make sense. How do we know where one letter ends and another letter begins? It's just a lot of numbers run together."

"I see what you mean," Jimmy said slowly. "I thought it was going to be keen, but I guess it won't work."

"Wait a minute!" Art interrupted. "Maybe it will. You don't use a zero in Braille, do you? The dots start with number one. If I wanted to spell 'Art' I would say, 'One, zero.' That's A."

"That's right," Jimmy agreed, "or we could use seven, eight, or nine, because they don't represent Braille dots either. Get out your alphabet cards and see if you can tell what I'm saying."

"Okay," said Chuck, reaching into his pocket for the card. "Take it slow."

Jimmy started. "One, four, seven."

"No," Chuck said, "there is no seven."

"That's what I'm telling you, dumbbell. One, four is C, and seven means that is the end of the C. Now let's go on. One, two, five, eight."

"Oh, I get it," said Chuck. "That's an H."

"One, three, six, nine," Jimmy continued.

"C-H-U . . . Hey, you're spelling my name," said Chuck.

"Sure," Jimmy said. "Now you both get busy and learn the alphabet."

"What comes at the end of a word?" Art asked.

"Two of the big numbers, or we can use the zero," Jimmy said.

"No," said Chuck. "We'll save the zero for the end of the sentence."

"Don't have to do that," said Jimmy. "We can use the period — two, five, six — at the end of a sentence."

"Let's see if I've got it," Chuck said. "One big number at the end of a letter and two big numbers at the end of a word."

"And a period at the end of a sentence," Jimmy added.

"We've got it, Jimmy!" Chuck sounded excited. "That's

super! It'll work and nobody will know what we're talking about."

"Let's try it out," Jimmy suggested. "I'll spell a word in our code and see who's the first to tell me what it is." He started spelling "S-e-a—"

"Sea," interrupted Art.

"No, I'm not finished," Jimmy said. "I didn't give you two big numbers to show the end of a word."

"Seam," said Chuck.

"It could be that," Jimmy said. "I was going to spell seal."

"Hey, I know that game," said Art. "Each one changes one letter and makes a different word. We've spelled 'seam' and 'seal.' Now I'll start a word."

Chuck and Art used their pencils, but Jimmy had to play the game in his head.

They were absorbed in their new game, not realizing they were teaching one another to read Braille, when Mrs. Carter came home.

"Hi, Mrs. Carter," said Chuck. "Gee, it must be getting late. I've got to get home."

"Wait a minute, Chuck." Jimmy stopped him, then turned to his mother. "Mom, I was thinking this morning," he started, "I've got that swell pitcher's glove and league bat that you and Carolyn gave me for my birthday." He stopped.

"Yes, I know," Mrs. Carter said.

"I won't ever use them again," Jimmy went on, "and they're too good not to be used."

"What had you thought of doing with them?" his mother asked.

"Would you and Carolyn mind if I gave them to Chuck and Art?"

"No, Jimmy. I think it would be a very nice thing to do."

"Wait a minute," said Art. "Hold everything! You can't do that."

"Mom says I can," Jimmy said quietly. "Chuck's got his catcher's mitt. My glove would be swell for you on second, Art."

"It would be keen, Jimmy, but I kinda hate to take it."

"Just don't teach it any bad habits, Art, like muffing a fly or a throw to second. And Chuck," Jimmy added, "don't you teach my bat to strike out."

Jimmy went to his room, followed by the two boys. He stood silent as the boys praised their gifts, Art trying on his glove, Chuck hefting the bat. He tried to smile as they thanked him, and then walked with them to the front door.

He stood there as they went out, and the door slammed as if closing on that part of his life. Another door barring him from the things he wanted to do, just as the closet door separated him from his Scout uniform. Could his guide dog open those doors for him? He wondered how.

Chapter
SEVEN

"HURRY UP, Miss Thompson!" Jimmy was waving an envelope and almost dancing in his excitement as he opened the door for her.

"What is it, Jimmy? What's happened?"

"It's my application from the guide-dog school."

"Oh, good!" Miss Thompson was almost as pleased as Jimmy.

"Mother left it for you to fill out," Jimmy explained.

She took the envelope. "We'll do it right away, and then we must call on the doctor."

"Another eye examination?" he asked.

"No, they want a complete physical checkup," she answered. "We know you're healthy, but they want the doctor's report."

"Oh, I see," said Jimmy.

"Now let's answer these questions." Together they went to the dining-room table, where Jimmy had been studying his Braille lesson. "Name, address, age," Miss Thompson began.

"Heck, you know all that!" Jimmy interrupted.

"Yes," she admitted, "but give me time to write it." Then she added, "You know, Jimmy, it is not customary for a guide-dog school to take an eleven-year-old boy."

"What do you mean?" Jimmy was worried.

"They're making an exception in your case because otherwise, with your mother working and Carolyn in school, you'd be alone all day."

"With my dog I won't be alone," Jimmy boasted.

"That's why they're doing this. Now here are some other things we have to answer. You promise not to be cruel to your dog, and agree to take good care of it."

"Sure," said Jimmy. "Of course I will."

They went on to fill out the blank and complete the routine questions. Later they visited the doctor.

The doctor poked and prodded, thumped and listened; he made Jimmy hop first on one foot and then on the other.

"Am I trying out for a track meet or going to the guide-dog school?" Jimmy grinned.

"You'll think it's both," the doctor said.

He made Jimmy stand with the toe of one foot at the heel of the other.

"What's this for?" Jimmy asked. "Must I learn to walk a tightrope?"

"Almost," the doctor explained. "You must have a good sense of balance. Your mind and your muscles must act quickly and together, as they do in playing basketball. You can't work with a guide dog and daydream about something else. If the school accepts you, you will find it interesting, but it's not easy."

"I won't mind anything if I get the dog," he promised.

"Well, I'll get this report off," the doctor said. "The school will notify you of their decision."

Jimmy sat tense as Miss Thompson drove him home, worrying about whether he had passed his tests. He could have hopped longer, if that was what they wanted. Was his balance all right? How could he joke with the doctor when he wanted the dog so much?

Then they were home. Miss Thompson parked in front of Jimmy's house. He got out and went thoughtfully indoors, wondering what it would be like when he had his dog to guide him.

During the days that followed Jimmy could hardly study his Braille; he kept thinking about what kind of dog he would get. His fingers ran over the Braille dots, but his mind saw dogs, running, jumping, and romping across the pages of his book.

Sometimes he helped Carolyn with her lessons when she read them aloud to him. He was surprised at how much of his own schoolwork he remembered. His mind was clearer, more active since he had lost his sight and had to depend on his memory for everything. Even so, the days dragged with the usual lonesomeness about the house.

One day he was especially lonesome, and was glad when the postman arrived to exchange a cheerful "Good morning," as Jimmy took the mail and laid it on the hall table. Just another bunch of bills, letters, and advertisements, he thought. "Oh well, I can't read 'em. Let 'em stay there till Mom comes home," he said aloud. "I think I'll take a walk around the block and get some fresh air and exercise."

Jimmy got his white cane and walked quickly to the corner, turned to the right, and surprised himself at the ease with which he covered the next block. He was going down the street parallel to the back of his house when he stubbed his cane. It flew out of his hand and clattered to the sidewalk. Jimmy stopped. "That's funny. I guess I wasn't holding it tight enough." He reached out with his foot to find the obstruction on the sidewalk, but the walk was smooth and clear.

"I don't get it," he said. "What did I bump into?" He stooped down and felt for his cane where he had heard it land, but it wasn't there. "Now that's where it fell," Jimmy told himself. "I heard it." He got down on hands and knees as if scrubbing the sidewalk, looking for the cane.

Jimmy was getting panicky. "It's got to be here. I've got to find it. How can I get home?" He searched over the width of the sidewalk from the curb to the lawn, then stood up.

"It didn't fall on the grass. I heard it hit the sidewalk, and it landed right here. I've got to get home." Jimmy held his hands in front of him and slid his feet along the pavement. His muscles were tense, and he was perspiring with strain and doubt. He swung his arms out, reaching for something — anything to hold onto — then stopped as something touched his leg. Here was a landmark. Jimmy reached down to clutch at it, but found nothing — just space and air. That might have been my cane, Jimmy thought. Somebody playing tricks.

"Hey, that ain't funny," he said aloud. "Give me back my cane. Haven't you got any sense?" Jimmy was getting angry. Some smart-aleck kid. He'd like to get his hands on him. Then the cane struck his shin again. He reached down quickly and grabbed it. "I ought to break it over your blockhead," he said to his unseen tormentor, but the cane was jerked again, almost out of his hands. "Let go," Jimmy shouted, "or I'll beat you with it!"

For answer he got a number of short jerks on the cane, accompanied by a playful growl. Jimmy's anger melted and he started to laugh. "Hey, you mutt," he scolded, "I'm not playing with you." But he jerked playfully at the cane, allowing the dog to make it a tug-of-war. He reached along the cane to the dog's head and scratched its ears. "You grabbed my cane, you rascal. It wasn't my fault at all. Just wait till I get my guide dog." He patted the dog. "I hope you'll be friends with him, dog." Jimmy took his cane and continued his walk. When he got home, the house somehow didn't seem so lonesome.

"Jimmy!" his mother called that evening as she was going through the mail. "Here's a letter for you from the guide-dog school."

Jimmy came running, bumping into the furniture in his hurry. "A letter? And it's just been lying there on the table all day?"

"Yes, but I'll read it to you now," his mother replied.

Jimmy heard the paper rattle as she opened the letter. "Hurry, Mom! Will they take me?"

"Just a minute, Jimmy."

"What's it say, Mom? Read it."

"Yes, you've been accepted. Oh, I'm so glad!"

"Oh boy! I get my dog." Jimmy was jumping up and down in his excitement.

"Now you won't be shut up in the house all day while I'm away," his mother said, reading the rest of the letter. "But wait a minute."

"What, Mom? What?"

"There are a lot of instructions, and you have only two weeks to get ready."

"Heck, I'm ready now."

"Not quite," she corrected him. "We'll have to go shopping. I'll have to get you some things. They sent a list."

"What sort of things?" Jimmy asked. "Mom, what?"

"Well, comfortable walking shoes."

"I've got them," Jimmy said. "What else?"

"I'll have to get you a raincoat and rubbers."

"Do I have to go out in the rain?"

"Yes, it seems the training doesn't stop for the weather," his mother said.

"When can we go shopping, Mom? Tomorrow?"

"Now don't be impatient, Jimmy. I'll take you Saturday afternoon."

"Hey, Midget!" Jimmy called. "I'm gonna get my dog. My letter has come."

"When?" Carolyn asked as she came in quickly.

"Just now. Mom just read it."

"I mean, when do you get your dog, and what's it like?" Carolyn was excited, too.

"Oh, not till I go to the school, and that won't be for two weeks," he said. "I don't know what it's like, but it's gonna be a swell dog."

"Can I pet it, Jimmy?" Carolyn asked.

"Sure, I guess so. Wait till I tell Art and Chuck."

"What're you gonna call it, Jimmy?"

"I don't know," he said. "Hey Mom, are you gonna take me to the school?"

"Can I go along?" Carolyn put in. "You can't leave me here all alone."

"I wish I could take you, Jimmy," Mrs. Carter said, "but the letter says the school wants you to travel alone."

"Me! Travel by myself? That's crazy!"

"No," his mother answered. "They want you to make the trip by yourself. It's a sort of test of your courage, Jimmy, and to show you the difference between traveling alone and traveling with your dog."

"Where is the school, Mommy?" Carolyn asked. "Will he go on the train?"

"It's about four hundred miles from here, and it will take all day," Mrs. Carter explained. "Miss Thompson suggested traveling by bus."

"And he's got to make that long trip all by himself?" Carolyn sounded worried.

"Gee! I couldn't go alone if I could see, much less this way."

"Don't worry, Jimmy." His mother laid her hand on his shoulder. "Miss Thompson has told me all about it, and you'll be perfectly safe."

"I don't know." Jimmy remembered what it was like just to cross the street.

Mrs. Carter hugged him. "Do you think I would let you go if there was any danger?"

"No, not if you knew it." Jimmy was imagining all sorts of things that might happen.

"Let us take care of it, Jimmy. I promise you will be all right."

Chapter
EIGHT

W<small>HEN</small> C<small>HUCK AND</small> A<small>RT</small> came over the next afternoon Jimmy told them about the letter from the school, and that he had to travel alone to get his dog. The boys were a little jealous of Jimmy. They didn't know whether to envy him more for traveling alone or for getting the dog.

"Did they tell you what kind of a dog you're gonna get?" Art asked. "I think you ought to get a Scotty."

"Oh no." Chuck waved that suggestion aside. "A Scotty is just a play dog. You want a collie."

"I guess I have to take what they give me," Jimmy said. "Miss Thompson told me that it's already trained."

"But what kind did they train?" Art asked.

"She didn't know what kind. But don't you worry, it's gonna be a swell dog." Jimmy was very confident.

"Yeah." Chuck was trying to be generous. "They wouldn't train just any old no-good dog. It would have to be smart."

"Sure," Art said, "and we can teach it to do tricks — to sit up, play dead dog, and maybe jump through a hoop."

Miss Thompson came in while the boys were talking. She was visiting Jimmy only once a week now to help with his advanced Braille. "Carolyn tells me you have been accepted at the school," she said to Jimmy. "I'm so glad for you."

"We're going to help Jimmy take care of the dog," Art told her.

"No, I'm afraid you won't," Miss Thompson said.

"How come?" asked Chuck.

"Don't be too disappointed if you can't play with it, boys," she explained. "It is a one-man dog, and has an important job to do."

"Can't I pet it?" Carolyn wanted to know.

"Jimmy will learn all the answers at the school," Miss Thompson answered. "When are you leaving, Jimmy?"

"I don't know. Mom hasn't told me. Two weeks from when the letter came."

"That's quite definite," Miss Thompson answered. "I probably won't be seeing you again until you come home, Jimmy, but you must let me know when you get back."

"Sure, Miss Thompson."

"I've enjoyed working with you, Jimmy," she added.

"Will the dog take over your job?" Chuck asked.

Miss Thompson laughed. "Yes, pretty much so, but I still want to keep in touch with you, Jimmy. Now I'll be going. I don't expect you to think about Braille at a time like this."

Jimmy took her to the door, while Carolyn and the two boys decided how they would build a doghouse and generally take care of Jimmy and his dog.

Aunt Martha loaned Jimmy a suitcase, and he paraded around the house carrying the empty suitcase during the day. Now he felt that he was really going away.

Saturday afternoon Jimmy went shopping with his

mother. It was the first time he had been downtown since his accident. He carried his white cane, but clung to his mother's arm, even while they were sitting in the street-car.

Now it was his turn to get the new outfit, his turn to walk "heavy" in a pair of new shoes, and to see how different the sidewalk felt under the stiff soles. His mother left him sitting in the clothing department while she went with the clerk to look at a suit for him.

Jimmy was listening to every sound around him. He heard footsteps and snatches of conversation as people passed him. Then he heard two ladies talking a little distance from him. "Look at that little boy," one of them said. "He's blind."

"Yes, I noticed," the other woman answered. "He has a bright little face. I wonder how old he is."

"If you're talking about me," Jimmy said, "I'm eleven."

"Well, what do you know about that?" the first woman said. "He heard us."

"Just because I can't see doesn't mean I can't hear." Jimmy scowled.

"I guess we were talking too loud. I hope we didn't hurt his feelings," one of them said as they walked away.

Jimmy was angry when his mother came back. "People talk about me as if I was a table or a post."

"They don't mean any harm, Jimmy. Here, try on this jacket." Jimmy soon forgot the two women in the excitement of getting a new suit.

Jimmy had no chance to get lonesome during the next week and the time for his trip came before he realized it.

Mrs. Carter gave a little going-away party with Aunt

Martha, Chuck, Art, and Carolyn. Aunt Martha gave
Jimmy an alarm clock that he could read with his fingers.

"See if you can tell what time it is, Jimmy," Aunt
Martha asked as she handed him the clock. "Be careful,
don't bend the hands. There's no glass over the face."

Jimmy took the clock and found a ring on the top and
two little feet on the bottom. "The twelve is up here,"
he said. "Hey, it's got Braille dots! But this a B."

"There are two dots at the twelve, three, six, and nine,"
Aunt Martha explained, "and one dot at each of the other
numbers."

"Gee, thanks, Aunt Martha. Now I won't have to ask
what time it is. That's swell." He carefully fingered the
face of the clock to read the time.

"Hey, Jimmy!" Chuck said. "How does it tell twelve
o'clock noon from twelve o'clock midnight?"

"Same as any other clock does, you dope. It doesn't
tell. I do."

Mrs. Carter gave Jimmy a "Braille slate." "Miss
Thompson helped me get this, Jimmy. You can write to
us on it. You put a piece of paper between these two
strips of metal and punch the Braille dots with this round
pointed nail — it's called a stylus. Then you mail the
paper home."

"That's keen, Mom. Hey, fellas, aren't you glad you
can read Braille?" Jimmy turned to his mother. "I wish
you had time to learn it, Mom."

"I'll teach you, Mommy," Carolyn promised. "I'm
getting along fine." Turning to Aunt Martha, she explained. "I don't read it with my fingers. I look at the
dots."

"That's wonderful, Carolyn. You can read Jimmy's letters to your mother."

"If he doesn't use any big words," Carolyn said.

"The important thing, Jimmy," Mrs. Carter interrupted, "is for you to use that Braille slate."

"Sure, Mom, and thanks a lot."

"I expect you to write home regularly on it, Jimmy. You know we'll miss you."

"Hey, how long will you be gone, Jimmy?" Chuck asked casually.

"Mom says I have to be at the school four weeks."

"Four weeks!" Chuck repeated. "Then this is a real going-away party."

"I didn't know it took that long to get a dog," Art said slowly.

"That's why Jimmy must write home regularly," Mrs. Carter said.

"I guess they'll have a study period, or a home-room period, when I can write letters." Jimmy had it all figured out.

"If you write to me, Jimmy, I'll pass the news on to Chuck and Art," his mother promised.

"I'll broadcast the news for you, Mommy," Carolyn said. " 'Station CC of the Carolyn Carter Broadcasting System, with the latest news report. We've just been handed a news flash that Mr. James Carter's dog chased a cat.' "

"How about that, Jimmy? What would you do if it saw a cat?" Chuck asked.

"I don't know," said Jimmy, "but all dogs don't chase cats."

"All right, children," Mrs. Carter broke in. "You just send me the news, Jimmy, and Carolyn will broadcast it. Remember I expect you to write regularly," she added.

Carolyn went to Jimmy with a small package wrapped in tissue paper and tied with a ribbon almost as big as the package. "I hope you like this, Jimmy." She handed the package to him.

Jimmy had some trouble untying it. This was different from shoelaces. He slipped the package out of the ribbon and unfolded the paper. "Gee, a handkerchief. That's swell, Midget."

"Feel the corner of it," Carolyn prompted. "I'm afraid it isn't very good."

Jimmy's fingers felt something raised. "Oh, it's an initial. Which is the right way up?"

"It's the same both ways," Carolyn said. "Look at it."

"Yeah. Two loops." Jimmy's fingers traced the raised outline. "It's a written J."

"Did you do that, Carolyn?" Aunt Martha asked.

"Yes," Mrs. Carter answered for Carolyn. "She's been working on it all of her spare time."

"Don't look at the under side," said Carolyn.

"The under side is all right," her mother praised. "You can be very proud of it, Carolyn."

Chuck poked a square paper box at Jimmy. "We didn't know what to get you, so Art and I decided to get this for the dog."

"What is it?" Jimmy asked, shaking it. "It rattles."

"It's dog biscuits," Art told him.

"That's very thoughtful of you boys," Mrs. Carter said. "I think Jimmy should save them until he comes home."

She was thinking of that large box fitting into the over-filled suitcase.

"Thanks, fellows," Jimmy said. "Yeah, Mom, I guess they will have food for the dog at the school. Gee, this is almost like Christmas."

After ice cream and cake, and more questions than anyone could answer, the boys went home and Jimmy went to bed. He tried to get some sleep, but kept on worrying about how he would manage for four long weeks away from home. He wanted the dog, but wished he didn't have to go alone to get it.

All night he was getting on and off buses, wondering how he would know the right one. He woke up, reached for his new clock and felt the hands, then remembered Aunt Martha had not shown him how to set the alarm. He hoped Mom would not let him oversleep.

Chapter

NINE

THE NEXT MORNING Mrs. Carter and Aunt Martha took Jimmy to the bus station.

Jimmy tried not to show how worried he was, and the excitement around him at the bus station helped to keep his mind away from the trip ahead of him.

He heard the announcer call the different buses over the loudspeaker while his mother and Aunt Martha were calmly talking together, their voices blending with the hum of confusion in the waiting room.

"Mom, why don't they call my bus?" Jimmy asked.

"It isn't time yet, Jimmy."

"But you're not listening, you're talking to Aunt Martha."

"Don't worry, Jimmy. We'll see that you don't get left," Aunt Martha assured him.

Just then a redcap came up to Mrs. Carter. "Your bus is ready now, ma'am," he said. "If you'll follow me, I'll take you to it."

"But they haven't called it yet," Jimmy protested. "I was listening."

"We take you out before it's called," the redcap explained, "to get ahead of the crowd."

"Come along, Jimmy," his mother said. "I'm putting your baggage check in the envelope with your ticket." She handed him the envelope. "Take good care of it."

"Mom, how will I know when to get off?"

"Don't worry about that." The redcap laughed. "They won't let you ride any farther than you paid for."

Jimmy clung to his mother as they went through the gate and out onto the loading platform, his white cane dangling, useless, at his side.

"Here's your passenger," the redcap called to a driver standing beside a bus.

Jimmy felt a strong hand grasp his arm. "All right, young man," the driver said. "Let me get you seated before the rush."

A quick hug and kiss from his mother and Aunt Martha, a breathless walk across the platform, then, half carried, half led, he stumbled up a couple of steps into the bus and felt himself being eased onto a soft cushion.

"You're sitting right behind me, fellow, where I can keep an eye on you. Now I've got to go out and collect my tickets," the driver told him, and Jimmy was alone in the large empty bus. He sat by a window, and as the passengers came into the bus Jimmy felt a man sit down beside him. "I guess that's your mother outside waving to you," he told Jimmy.

"Where?" Jimmy asked.

"Right over there," the man pointed.

Jimmy waved as the bus started, but he didn't know in which direction he should wave. He sat very tense, very straight in his seat, gripping his white cane as tightly as he had the first time he crossed the street.

The bus had gone just a short distance when the man beside Jimmy asked, "Do you make this trip often?"

"No sir. I've never traveled alone before, but the school says I have to."

A lady in the seat behind them had overhead. "But isn't that dangerous, young man? Why must you do that?"

"It's one of the rules of the school," Jimmy explained. "The bus driver promised to take care of me."

"Are you going to the school for the blind?" she asked.

"Heck, no. I'm going to the guide-dog school. I'm going to get a dog," Jimmy said proudly.

The lady turned to a passenger across the aisle. "This young man is going to a guide-dog school and is traveling all by himself. Isn't that wonderful?"

"How far are you going?" one of the passengers asked.

"About four hundred miles," Jimmy answered. "I won't get there until night."

"What's your name?" another passenger asked.

"I'm Jimmy Carter," he said. And from then on the bus adopted him.

The general conversation was interrupted when they stopped for lunch and the driver turned to him. "If you'll come with me, we'll go to the lunchroom."

"We'll take him with us," several of the passengers said, and Jimmy found himself the center of a friendly group of people who had not known one another before. They all wanted to order for him.

"I think I'd like a hamburger," Jimmy said, "and a glass of milk."

"Bring him two hamburgers," the voice next to him ordered.

"Wait a minute!" Jimmy was confused. "How much will all this cost?"

"You're my guest," several said at once, and then argued with one another about it.

"Thank you," said Jimmy, "but Mother gave me expense money."

"How do you handle money?" someone asked Jimmy. "How can you tell a one-dollar bill from a ten?"

"I can't," Jimmy said, "but I'm not supposed to carry anything larger than a five, so the change will be in ones, and I fold them different."

"That's clever. But how do you recognize change?"

"Oh, that's easy," said Jimmy. "Half-dollars, quarters, and dimes are rough around the edge. A nickel is kind of like a quarter, but smooth around the edge. And you won't mix pennies and dimes, because the edge of the penny is smooth."

"I never noticed that," one of the men said, and they all dug into their pockets to discover if they could tell what coins they had by the feel of them.

"You keep your money in your pocket," someone told Jimmy. "I've got your check."

"Thank you ever so much, sir."

"All aboard," the driver shouted, and Jimmy was led back to the bus and showered with more candy bars than were good for him.

The trainer was at the station to meet Jimmy. "I'm Mr. Weeks from the school," he said. "I suppose you are Mr. James Carter."

"Did you bring my dog?" was Jimmy's first question.

Mr. Weeks laughed. "Not yet. There's a lot to do before you get the dog."

"Oh!" Jimmy was disappointed, but had no time to show it.

"Take my arm and we'll go to the station wagon," Mr. Weeks said. "We'll drive out to the school."

Jimmy was going to know that station wagon very well.

"Did you have any trouble on the trip, Mr. Carter?"

Jimmy listened for someone to answer. Then, after a pause, "Oh, you mean me? I'm Jimmy."

"No. You are Mr. Carter while at the school," Mr. Weeks explained. "You see most of our students feel helpless and dependent because they are newly blind. By treating them with respect, we make them feel like grown men and women again."

"And everybody calls me Mister?" Jimmy asked.

"Just the members of the school staff. The students may call one another by their first names."

Jimmy settled back in his seat. His lips moved. "Mister Carter" he almost whispered. It sounded good, and he felt very grown-up.

When they arrived at the school, Mr. Weeks took Jimmy's suitcase and led him up a short flight of stairs into a wide hall.

"Oh, Mr. McDonald," he called to someone standing there. "This is Mr. James Carter. He's your roommate. Will you take his suitcase and show him around? I have some other things I must do."

Jimmy felt a strong handclasp as a deep voice said, "Hello, Jim, glad to know you. Call me Mack. Come along and I'll take you to our room."

Jimmy was led down the hall and into their bedroom.

"This is my bed," Mack explained. "Yours is by the window. Give me your hand. This is your chest of drawers."

Jimmy felt his hand laid gently on a piece of furniture. Before he had time to inspect it, Mack tucked Jimmy's arm under his own and started across the room.

"I'll Braille the room for you. Your closet is next to

mine, and there are coat hangers in it. Here it is. You can look at it later. This next door leads to our bathroom, and this door over here leads outside to a fenced-in runway for our dogs. Here's a window. Now you're back to your chest of drawers again. Your chair is between it and your bed. I put your suitcase on your bed. You had better unpack and put your things away. I'll come for you when the dinner gong rings. You've got about an hour."

"Well, w-e-l-l." Jimmy's mind was spinning. "Who's going to help me unpack?"

"You'd better do that for yourself," Mack advised. "How can you find your clothes if someone else puts them away?"

Jimmy felt very lost, very much alone, and for the first time since he had started to work with Miss Thompson he felt very, very blind. "Can't you at least show me what to do?" he asked.

"What do you want to know?" Mack inquired. "Put your shirts in the second drawer, your underwear in the third drawer; hang your clothes in the closet, and use the top drawer for your handkerchiefs, socks, and small items. And, oh yes, put your toothpaste on the third shelf in the medicine cabinet. I'm using the second shelf from the bottom for mine. Put your shaving cream and razor to the left on the bottom shelf."

"Razor?" Jimmy questioned.

"Sure," Mack said. "What do you use, electric or safety?"

"Not — not either one. You're kidding me," Jimmy said. "I — I don't shave yet."

"Well, you're lucky. How old are you?" Mack asked.

"I'm eleven, going on twelve," Jimmy said. "How old are you?"

"I'm twenty-eight," Mack replied. "Now you better get busy and put your things away. You can do that, can't you?"

"Not without help," Jimmy stammered. "You seem to forget I'm blind."

"Well," Mack said quietly, "what do you think I am?"

Then Jimmy realized that this confident, steady chap was also blind.

When the gong rang for dinner, Mack rescued Jimmy, who was still struggling with his unpacking. Jimmy dumped the things into the chest of drawers and put the empty suitcase on the floor of his closet.

Mack led him into the dining room, and Jimmy remembered some of the things Miss Thompson had taught him about feeling the size of a room. He heard footsteps coming from quite a distance on the linoleum-covered floor, and the sound of those footsteps bounced back from walls that seemed far apart.

"This is a large room," Jimmy said to himself.

His thoughts were interrupted as Mack put Jimmy's hand on the back of a chair. "This is your place," Mack told him. "I'm across the table from you."

The footsteps Jimmy had heard approaching now reached the end of the table, and a chair scraped on the floor as someone sat down. "I'm Mr. Weeks, your trainer," the voice said from that end of the table. He introduced the students, and Jimmy learned that there were seven other men and two girls, Dorothy Blake and Shirley Scott, in the class.

By this time a plate had been quietly laid on the table in front of Jimmy, and he waited for someone to cut up his food as his mother had done. He heard the rest of the blind students eating, laughing, and talking.

Miss Young, the social secretary, came over to Jimmy's side. "What's the matter, Mr. Carter? You aren't eating."

"Mother always cut up my food," he answered.

"You will learn to do that for yourself," she told him. "Let me show you. We use the face of a clock for directions."

"Oh, I know about that," Jimmy said.

"Good. Now take your fork and I will hold your hand. Your slice of meat is down here at six o'clock." Guiding his hand, she touched the meat with the tip of his fork. "Your mashed potatoes are at nine o'clock, here. The carrots are from two to four o'clock over here, and string beans are up at twelve o'clock." She touched each vegetable with his fork as she spoke. "Your salad is in a small dish at nine o'clock, your bread-and-butter plate is at eleven, and your glass of water at twelve o'clock."

Nora, the cook, came in to inquire who wanted coffee, tea, or milk. Jimmy was tempted to take coffee. He wanted to be grown-up, but realized his mother would not approve. So he chose the milk, and Miss Young explained, "Nora will put the milk at one o'clock next to your plate."

Miss Young showed him how to cut the meat for himself and then went back to her own place at the table. The knife felt awkward in Jimmy's hand; he wasn't sure whether he was cutting with the sharp or the dull edge. He turned it over and then turned it back again. Both

edges seemed dull — or else the meat was tough. Finally
he got a bit cut off and started to lift it up, only to
find that he had put an empty fork into his mouth.
Jimmy hoped nobody was looking, and then remembered
that the rest of the students were blind also. He fished
around gently until his fork came in contact with a piece
of meat; he started to lift it, and this time the whole slice
came up. Little beads of perspiration formed at the back
of his neck and began to run like a miniature Niagara
Falls down his spine. He felt nervous and flustered. Holding the meat firmly with his fork, he stabbed at it, making a powerful thrust with his knife. His plate tilted
forward and the slice of meat slid into his lap.

Jimmy was horrified. "What will I do now?" he asked
himself. "Shall I sneak it back to my plate or wrap it up
in my napkin and pretend that I've eaten it?" He wished
he were back at home where his mother could fuss over
him. Then he heard Miss Young at his side.

"Don't let that bother you, Mr. Carter," she said so
quietly that no one else could hear. "That can happen just
as easily to people who can see. Many a person carving
a Thanksgiving turkey has had the turkey fly across the
table."

She gathered up Jimmy's napkin with the slice of meat
in it and again said quietly, "Eat your vegetables until I
get back." He heard her footsteps fade down the length
of the room toward the kitchen door.

Jimmy ate his vegetables. The mashed potatoes were
easy, but the string beans tried to play a game with him.
If he tried to scoop them up on his fork, they slid off, and
time after time he brought an empty fork to his mouth.

He decided to spear them, and they stuck to his fork like jackstraws sticking out at various angles. As he brought the fork to his mouth, one of the beans struck his upper lip, one dribbled against his chin, and a couple stuck out like fingers at either side of his mouth. Jimmy wished he had a funnel or a megaphone. He wondered how the other students were able to eat and laugh and talk at the same time without washing their faces in vegetable juice.

He thought of Mack and of how capable he was, then said to himself, "They've all been blind longer and had more training than I have."

Miss Young returned with a fresh slice of meat and again showed Jimmy how to measure off a bite size, cut it, and bring it up to his mouth. He didn't know how much of his food slid off his plate onto the table while he was eating. Miss Young didn't tell him, and the blind students never knew. He made up his mind that he, too, would learn to eat nicely. But there were so many things he had to learn!

Chapter
TEN

AFTER DINNER the class was assembled in the recreation room, where Mr. Weeks gave them the first of their many lectures. He took their white canes away from them, explaining, "You won't need these canes now, because you will have your dogs to see for you."

Jimmy was reluctant to give up his cane. It was the symbol of his first step toward adjustment to his blindness, and learning to use it had cost him much time and effort. It had become a companion, something solid to hold to give him courage when crossing a busy traffic intersection. His white cane was a part of him.

"I'd like to keep my cane, if I may," he told Mr. Weeks.

"Miss Young will mail it home if you wish," Mr. Weeks said, "but you'll never use it again."

Jimmy wasn't so sure, and he asked Miss Young to send it home for him.

"Your dog will wear a harness with a stiff leather U-shaped handle that you will hold when the dog is guiding you," Mr. Weeks said, going on with his lecture, "and a leash is attached to the dog's collar so that you can control your dog when you drop the handle. Both of these are held in your left hand, and your dog will always work on your left. This leaves your right hand free to carry a package, open doors, make change, or do any of the number of things for which you need your hands."

Jimmy went to bed early that night, and was routed out at six o'clock the next morning for a seven-o'clock breakfast. He wasted a good deal of time finding his clothes, and Mack explained to him that if he put his shoes and the rest of his clothes in a certain place, and remembered where they were, he could find them more easily.

After breakfast the class again assembled in the recreation room.

"We are going for a walk down the highway," Mr. Weeks told them. "I want you to assemble here in half an hour, ready for your first lesson in training. You've all been instructed to bring comfortable walking shoes."

Jimmy was wearing the shoes in which he had traveled to the school. Now he had to find where he had put his other pair. There were only three drawers in the chest of drawers, and he looked through all three; then he looked in his suitcase.

"Mack," he called to his roommate, "do you think anyone could have moved my shoes?"

"I told you to put your things where you could find them. No, your shoes have not been moved. Nora has been around blind people for a number of years, and when she straightens up the room she puts everything back exactly where it was. She wouldn't put a pin from one side of the dresser to the other."

"I wonder where my shoes are?" Jimmy was thinking out loud.

"They're right where you put 'em. Look under the bed. Are they in your suitcase? Are you sure you brought them?"

"Yes." Jimmy answered with his head and shoulders under the bed.

"Then look on the floor of the closet," Mack suggested.

"I'll bet that's where they — ouch!" Jimmy had tried to stand up before he was clear of the bed. He found the shoes and then straggled into the recreation room.

Mr. Weeks took the class out the back door. He had a long rope with handles tied to it about three feet apart. He put five students on the right and five on the left of this rope, each holding onto a handle.

"This is like Swiss mountain climbing," he told them, "only we're walking on level ground."

"I don't get it," Jimmy said half aloud.

"You will," Shirley told him from the opposite side of the rope, "and you'll get it good."

"I want you all to walk briskly," Mr. Weeks was saying. "I'm holding the front end of the rope, but don't hang back and make me drag you. I'm neither a horse nor a tractor. Our first walk will be a half mile down the highway; then we'll turn around and come back to the school. Are we all ready?"

They all thought so, or guessed so, but didn't sound very enthusiastic.

"Let's go!" Mr. Weeks shouted, and they found themselves half walking, half trotting down the road. Jimmy had not realized how much he had slowed down since his accident. It felt strange to be moving so quickly through the darkness, almost as if he were a spaceship, headed for nowhere and traveling through nothing. He was beginning to tire from the fast pace, and he could hear heavy breathing around him.

"Come on," shouted Mr. Weeks. "Lift your feet."

Jimmy was just about to give up. He was afraid to complain, afraid they might not let him get his dog. The same thought seemed to be in the minds of the others. There were murmurings, but no outright protests.

Finally Mr. Weeks stopped. "All right," he called to them. "We'll stop now and let you get your breath, then we will start back."

"We won't have to walk back as fast as we came out, will we?" Shirley pleaded.

"What's the matter? You're not tired, are you?" Mr. Weeks asked her. "You haven't been walking, I've been dragging you, and you better keep moving on the way back or you'll have to drop out of line."

"That's no punishment," Shirley told him.

"How will you find your way back?" he asked. "But then if you drop out, you won't need to go back to the school."

"Oh," Shirley said quietly, and Jimmy understood what Mr. Weeks meant. They were not going to be babied just because they were blind.

They started back at the same pace at which they had come out. Everyone was puffing, staggering, and walking a little way, then breaking into a jog trot. At last they stopped at the back door of the school.

"All right," Mr. Weeks told them. "That's all for this morning. It's ten o'clock, and you have two hours before lunch. I guess all of you want a shower and rest."

"I'm dead," Shirley murmured. "I hope my dog won't walk like that."

Jimmy ached in muscles he'd forgotten he had. When Mack came out of the shower, Jimmy couldn't decide whether he wanted to clean up or just lie there. "I don't get it, Mack. What was all this for?"

"To get the kinks out of your legs," Mack answered.

"Will our dogs walk as fast as that?"

"Of course not. This is just to find out if you will be able to work with a dog," Mack explained, "and to get you limbered up so that you won't drag on him."

"I don't know, Mack. They may find out that I can't keep up." Jimmy rubbed the aching calf of his leg.

"You did all right this morning," Mack encouraged.

"That was once. Maybe I couldn't do it again." Jimmy was worried. "Mack, what will happen if I can't get my dog?"

"Quit worrying about it." Then Mack asked, "Ever play baseball all afternoon?"

Jimmy didn't answer. His mind flashed back to the last time he had played baseball — to the time Mike Adams threw a giant firecracker in his face and started all this. That was the last time he had run, the last time he had ever walked so quickly — until today. "Okay, Mack," he said, getting up. "I guess I'll take my shower."

That afternoon they repeated the walk they had taken in the morning, only this time it didn't seem quite so bad.

The next morning Jimmy went for a solo walk with Mr. Weeks. He was given one end of a handle like the one a guide dog wears on his harness, and Mr. Weeks held the other end.

"There are three basic commands," he told Jimmy. "Forward, right, and left. I will pretend to be the dog, and we will try the commands. Now if you say 'Forward,' I'll go forward."

Jimmy gave the command. Mr. Weeks led Jimmy forward a few steps and then stopped.

"What are we stopping for?" Jimmy asked.

"The dog won't tell you." Mr. Weeks laughed. "Reach out with your foot and see."

Jimmy reached out his foot and said, "Oh, we're at the curb."

"Yes. Now you must thank the dog," the trainer told him. "Say, 'That's a good dog.' It's the only pay he gets for his work. Then be ready to step down from the curb and again give the command 'Forward.'"

They crossed the street, and again Mr. Weeks stopped.

"Now what?" Jimmy asked.

"Put out your foot and find out every time the dog stops," Mr. Weeks explained. "He will stop for any uneven place in the sidewalk or anywhere that you might trip or stumble."

"Oh, we're across the street." Jimmy's foot had found the curb.

"Remember to thank your dog every time he does a good job, before you give him the next command," Mr. Weeks said. "Now put your foot up on the curb and again say 'Forward.' Take two steps and say 'Left,' and your dog will turn left."

They practiced for about an hour over the obstacle course, with Mr. Weeks playing guide dog. Jimmy said afterward that Mr. Weeks did everything but bite. "He growled once in a while when I made a silly mistake, but it was a lot of fun. I can't wait to get my dog."

After three days of practice Jimmy was sent to the recreation room, where Mr. Weeks seated him in a chair near the door, gave him a leash, and put some meat in Jimmy's left hand.

The meat felt cold and moist. "Is this for the dog?" Jimmy asked.

"That's right," Mr. Weeks answered. "When the dog comes in, sit quietly and let him sniff around the room. When he comes to you for the meat, snap this leash onto his collar. Do you understand? Your dog's name is Sirius."

Jimmy nodded with a quick little jerk of his head; he was breathing rapidly, and the hand that held the meat trembled. Mr. Weeks left the room and Jimmy sat tense, straining his ears to listen. A few moments later he heard the door open and the dog's toenails clicking on the floor as it ran around the room. He wondered how big the dog was and what it looked like. The clicking stopped in front of him, and Jimmy could almost see the dog looking at him. Slowly he reached out the hand that held the meat and felt a moist, soft muzzle very carefully taking the meat from his hand. He snapped the leash to the chain collar and hugged the dog.

Mr. Weeks came in. "Well, what do you think of your dog?"

Jimmy could hardly talk. "He's — he's wonderful!"

"When I met you at the bus, you asked me if I had your dog," Mr. Weeks reminded him. "Now you've got it."

Jimmy's hands were going over the dog, feeling the

soft fur of its ears, the long slender muzzle. He turned his face toward Mr. Weeks, still fondling the dog. "What — what does he look like?"

"He's a pedigreed German shepherd, black with a tan underbody and legs. From now on you must take care of him, groom him every day with a currycomb and brush, and only you must feed him. It is important that no stranger should ever feed your dog. Now you take Sirius to your room and get acquainted. Tomorrow we'll try him in harness."

Jimmy gathered up the leash and started for his room to show Mack his dog. He paraded down the hall with the dog trotting by his side like a circus performer. All he needed was a brass band and a ringmaster.

The next day Jimmy and three other students with their dogs were driven to a quiet section of town, where Jimmy walked beside his dog, holding the harness as he had when walking with Mr. Weeks. The dog went very fast, and Jimmy had trouble keeping up with it. Halfway down the block he bumped into something. Without stopping, he said, "Oh, I beg your pardon," and went on. Then he realized he had bumped into a post.

"Hold it, Mr. Carter," Mr. Weeks called.

"We just bumped into a post," Jimmy explained.

"I know. Your dog shouldn't do that. If he bumps you again, scold him."

At lunch all the students related their experiences of the morning. Jimmy told about bumping into the post.

"Be careful about knocking down our trees and telephone posts," Mr. Weeks told them. "We need them to train the next class."

In the days that followed, Jimmy's walks were extended and became more varied, going into busier sections of the city.

"I advise you to cross busy streets only where there are traffic signals," Mr. Weeks instructed, "and you must watch for the green light. You know all dogs are color-blind."

"Maybe that's why Sirius bumped me into that post," Jimmy said. "It must have been colored."

Mr. Weeks laughed. "Then you better listen for colored posts and traffic lights."

One day Sirius stopped as they were going down the sidewalk. Jimmy reached out with his foot. He was sure there was no curb there, but something was wrong. He put out his hand and everything seemed clear, so he said "Forward." The dog took one step forward and stopped again. Jimmy didn't know what to do. Mr. Weeks came to his side.

"What's the matter, Mr. Carter?"

"I don't know. Sirius won't go."

"Then find out why," Mr. Weeks told him.

"I did. I asked Sirius, but he wouldn't tell me. There seems to be nothing in the way."

"There must be," Mr. Weeks insisted, "or the dog wouldn't stop."

Jimmy reached out his hand again and found a board across the sidewalk, resting on two boxes. The dog could have walked under the board, but Jimmy would have bumped into it.

Then Jimmy was taught how to go around all obstacles that block sidewalks — cars, bicycles, or even toys carelessly left there. Around these Sirius guided him expertly. Every day Jimmy grew more proud of his four-legged eyes. When the dog was leading him, it was almost as if he could see again.

He was having trouble with the dog's name. One day he told Mr. Weeks, "That name isn't good enough for my dog."

"But that is the most honored name a dog could have," Mr. Weeks told him. "Don't you know who Sirius was?"

"Why, no. Was there really somebody by that name?"

"It's in a legend in Greek mythology," Mr. Weeks explained. "Sirius was a dog who belonged to the giant hunter Orion. Sirius never left his master, and went with him on all of his hunting trips. Orion was a friend of Artemis, goddess of the hunt. One day Artemis accidentally shot Orion with an arrow, and then felt so sorry that she had him taken up into the heavens and made into the constellation of Orion. Sirius grieved for his master so much that Artemis had him placed in the heavens also. He is the Dog Star at the heel of the constellation of Orion in the southern hemisphere. The Dog Star is the brightest star in the heavens, and is twenty times brighter than our sun."

"Then why don't we get light from it like we do from the sun?" Jimmy wanted to know.

"Why, Mr. Carter," Mr. Weeks said. "You know that it is too far from our earth. The sun is only ninety-three million miles, in round numbers, and Sirius is about eight and a half light-years away."

"What's a light-year?" Jimmy asked.

"A light-year is the distance it takes a beam of light to

travel in a year, and light travels one hundred eighty-six thousand, two hundred and seventy miles a second."

"That's almost two hundred thousand miles a second." Jimmy was thinking out loud. "And there are an awful lot of seconds in a year. No wonder we don't get sunburned from that star."

"But in a way we do," Mr. Weeks said.

"What! Get sunburned from a star?" Jimmy asked.

"The Dog Star rises and sets with the sun during July and August. Those are called dog days and are the hottest part of the year, so you see the Dog Star does affect our sunburn. Your dog was named Sirius after the Dog Star."

Jimmy was not impressed. "That's not a good name for him. Sirius always *followed* Orion, but my dog goes ahead and shows the way. I'd like to call him Leader."

"You may change it after you get home," Mr. Weeks said, "but here you must use his pedigree-registered name."

"You'll be my leader, whatever they call you, won't you?" Jimmy hugged the dog. "Think you can keep me out of trouble and take me where I want to go?"

Chapter
ELEVEN

ONE MORNING Mr. Weeks knocked on their door at six o'clock, and when Mack and Jimmy answered, he went away.

"It's your turn to shower first, Jim," Mack called.

"You can have first turn, Mack." Jimmy yawned sleepily. He wanted a few extra winks in bed.

"Okay. It will give me more time to shave." Mack hopped out of bed and hurried into the bathroom. Half asleep, Jimmy heard him splashing and singing under the shower. He thought Mack came out and started dressing, but he was still only half awake.

"Where are you, Jim? I don't hear you," Mack called. "It's just too bad if you've gone back to sleep."

Now Jimmy was wide awake. He didn't know how much time he had wasted, and the breakfast gong might sound any minute. He dashed into the bathroom, snapped open the medicine cabinet to get his toothpaste, and squeezed a ribbon of it onto his index finger. That was the way he measured the amount to use. Then he grabbed his toothbrush, spread the paste on the brush, and started scrubbing his teeth. It tasted strange; it was strong, and there were no bubbles. He didn't know what he had gotten hold of, but it certainly wasn't his tooth-paste. He rinsed out his mouth and called, "What kind of toothpaste do you use, Mack?"

"I don't know the name," Mack answered. "Why? Are you out? Mine is on the second shelf."

Jimmy realized his toothpaste should be on the third shelf and he had taken the tube from the bottom shelf. Again he called to Mack. "What's in this tube on the bottom shelf?"

Mack came to the bathroom door. "That's my brush-less shave cream, you chump, and don't you waste it."

"I wonder if it will make me sick," Jimmy said. "I tried to brush my teeth with it."

Mack laughed. "Oh, it won't hurt you, but I'll bet it didn't taste good. Hurry and get your things on, or you'll be late for breakfast."

Of course Mack told about it at the breakfast table, and the rest of the students had a good laugh at Jimmy's expense.

"Don't you have your toothpaste marked, Mr. Carter?" Miss Young asked.

"What do you mean, marked?"

"All of your things are marked, aren't they?" she asked.

"Well, there's a laundry mark, but I can't read it."

"No. I mean each article." Miss Young turned to the other students at the table and asked what system each one used for marking his clothes.

Shirley used very small safety pins placed where they would not show — one pin on the bottom of each of her white blouses and two pins on the colored ones. She arranged the pins in such a way as to recognize the colors of her clothes. She did the same with her dresses and suits. Her blue suit had two pins fastened in an X under the coat label and also on the inside of the skirt waistband. She used two pins set parallel on her brown suit.

One of the boys had his clothes marked in Braille, using French knots for the Braille dots. Mack marked things with dress snaps because they have little bumps on them, just like the Braille letters. Dorothy used bobby pins.

Each student had his own system, and Miss Young promised to help Jimmy mark his things as soon as he decided what system he wanted to use.

"I pin my stockings together in pairs," Shirley said, "so that I won't wear one light and one dark stocking at the same time."

"That gives me an idea," Jimmy said. "I could tie my shoelaces together to keep my shoes matched up. I went out once wearing one black and one brown shoe."

"The trouble is, Jimmy," Dorothy teased, "you're color-blind, like our dogs."

The after-breakfast chat was interrupted by Mr. Weeks, who ordered the class out for their morning trip. They piled into the station wagon with their dogs and were driven to the city. When they arrived, Mr. Weeks sent them out in couples and told them to meet at a coffee shop about eight or ten blocks away for mid-morning coffee and doughnuts. This was a test of memory. He gave each pair of students a different route that would bring them to the coffee shop.

Jimmy and Dorothy started out together. At the first corner they had their first argument.

"We turn to the right here," Jimmy told her.

"No," Dorothy insisted, "we go down another block and then cross the street."

"Okay, we'll go your way," Jimmy agreed after Dorothy convinced him that she was right. "How are we supposed to remember all this?"

"You'll have a route of twenty blocks to remember before you graduate," Dorothy said.

"How do you know?" Jimmy asked.

"A friend of mine has a dog. She gave me some tips."

They finally arrived at the coffee shop, where the rest of the class were assembled. As they ate their doughnuts and coffee, the students related their experiences, laughing over them and blaming the mistakes on their partners.

When they finished eating, Mr. Weeks sent them back to the station wagon, giving them all the same route but having each one leave alone, about five minutes apart. When Jimmy's turn came, he started out bravely with Sirius. He knew the route by heart. He knew just which corners to turn and which streets to cross.

After walking for what seemed a very long time, he heard a group of children at play in a schoolyard. Jimmy remembered the school, but it was in the opposite direction from where the station wagon was parked. He turned around to go back toward the station wagon. In the middle of the second block he stopped. "That smells like the paint store," he said to himself, "but it shouldn't be there." He tried to figure out just what had happened. "That might not be the paint store," he argued. "It could be someone painting a house."

Jimmy didn't want to admit that he might be lost. If

this was the paint store, a bakery should be near the end of the block. He gave Sirius the command "Forward," and went down the block, sniffing at each doorway he passed, but he did not smell the bakery. At the corner he turned around and walked back. He wondered what Sirius was thinking of this strange behavior.

He listened for footsteps, but everything seemed quiet, although he could hear cars going past. Jimmy knew he was away from the center of town. What must he do? Where had he taken the wrong turn? How could it have happened? He was confused and worried. Then he heard the click of a woman's high heels and started toward the sound.

"Can I help you, young man?" the lady asked.

"Yes, please," Jimmy said. "I think I'm lost. I want to get to Fifth and E Streets."

"You're quite a ways from there. You'll have to go back this way," she said.

"Which way is 'this way'?" Jimmy asked.

"Over here," the woman pushed him a little way. Jimmy didn't know in which direction.

"If you will face me in the right direction my dog will take me," Jimmy said. The woman turned him around. "Thank you very much," Jimmy said. "How did you know I was lost?"

"That gentleman across the street sent me," she whispered. "But I think he doesn't want you to know it."

The lady went on, and Jimmy started in the direction she had indicated. He knew it must be Mr. Weeks across the street, but there was nothing he could do about it now. He walked a couple of blocks and again heard the children playing in the schoolyard. Now he was completely lost. He dropped the handle of the dog's harness and tried to feel from which direction the sun was shining by turning his face to feel the heat.

Mr. Weeks came up to him. "What's the matter, Mr. Carter?" he asked. "Are you in trouble?"

"You know I am," Jimmy said. "I'm lost. I can't get away from this school. I left it a few blocks away and now I'm back to it."

"This is a different school," Mr. Weeks told him. "Probably that's what confused you."

He guided Jimmy to the station wagon, where the rest of the class was waiting. All the way back to the guide-dog school they teased Jimmy about being an explorer.

"Jimmy didn't get lost," Mack explained. "It was the station wagon that was lost."

At the school, Jimmy and Mack went to their room to rest and then clean up for lunch. Jimmy was still worried over getting lost.

"Don't let it bother you, Jim," Mack told him. "I took the wrong turn myself and would have gotten off the course, but I heard Dorothy across the street talking to her dog. I had walked faster and caught up with her. Then I trailed her to the station wagon."

"I bet they all get lost sometimes," Jimmy said.

"Sure," Mack agreed. "You're doing swell. I took a spill on Fourth Street — that rough place on the sidewalk."

"Oh, I know," Jimmy said. "Where the pavement is broken. Did you hurt yourself?"

"Yeah, my dignity," Mack answered. "I don't know who was watching, but if you tell on me I'll break your neck."

"What did Smoky do when you fell?"

"Just came up and licked my face."

"Did you ever have a pet dog, Mack?" Jimmy asked.

"Yes, when I could see," Mack said. "Funny, I was thinking about that the other day."

"I never had a dog before," Jimmy said.

"I had a bull terrier," Mack told him, "but we were not as close as Smokey and I are. You see, a pet dog is with you just a little while in the morning before work and again in the evening, but Smoky is almost a part of me, aren't you, mutt?" He turned to the dog.

Smoky, hearing his name, had come over to the side of the bed and nuzzled at Mack's hand. Mack lay there resting, scratching the dog's ear and worrying its muzzle with his fist while Smoky gnawed his hand playfully.

"I think I know why I got lost," Jimmy said. "There was an automobile in the way, and we had to walk around it to cross the street. Guess we went the wrong way."

"You have to watch for that, Jim. Cars often stand in the crosswalk waiting for a signal. You can't walk in front of them or you'll be in the line of traffic, and you shouldn't walk behind them because they might back up."

"Did you ever drive a car, Mack?"

"Yes, when I could see. Why?"

"What sort of examination did they give you to get a license?"

"Why, you fill out a questionnaire, read some letters on a chart to test your eyesight, and then drive around with the examiner so he can tell if you know how to handle the car — parking and going up hills and that kind of thing."

"You mean I had to take a harder examination for my

guide dog than a person takes to get a driver's license?"

Mack laughed. "I never heard it put that way, but I'm afraid you're right, Jim. I sometimes think there are more blind people driving automobiles than using guide dogs."

"Hey, it must be lunchtime, Mack. Are you ready?" Jimmy was hungry.

"Just about," Mack answered. "Wonder where we'll go this afternoon."

That night Jimmy stretched out comfortably in his bed and fell asleep. Suddenly he awoke. He had been awakened by someone touching or shaking his bed, so he kept still for a moment, waiting to see what it was all about. Everything was quiet. He could hear Mack's steady breathing in the other bed, and he wondered what woke him up. Then he heard his dog breathing softly, and he laughed at himself as he went back to sleep. Sirius slept under the bed, and Jimmy couldn't move without Sirius' knowing it. When Jimmy turned over in bed the dog woke up, and when Sirius turned over he bumped the springs and Jimmy woke up. That made it fifty-fifty. Sirius had turned over.

The next morning Jimmy had a letter to mail home, and Mr. Weeks showed him the mailbox in the recreation room. "Give me your hand," he said. "Look at this sharp corner on the mantelpiece. Watch out for that. It is just the height of your face."

Jimmy touched the sharp point and drew back. "That's dangerous," he said.

"That's why I showed it to you," Mr. Weeks said.

"Seems to me you could put a piece of sponge rubber on that corner," Jimmy went on, "specially when there are blind people who could get hurt on it."

"We could," Mr. Weeks answered; then asked quietly, "Mr. Carter, do you expect the world to pad its corners for you just because you're blind?"

"Oh," Jimmy said slowly. "I see what you mean." He reached down and scratched Sirius' ear. "You'll keep me from bumping into sharp corners, won't you!" And the dog rubbed his head against Jimmy's knees as if understanding and agreeing to the promise.

Just then the breakfast gong sounded and Jimmy went into the dining room, where the rest of the class was gathering. He found his own chair, and Sirius found his own place under the table.

Miss Young helped Nora bring in the breakfast plates. Mr. Weeks explained they were having hot cakes and sausage. While he was speaking, Miss Young called Mr. Weeks to answer the telephone. He excused himself and left the table, leaving the students alone.

By that time everyone was served, and Jimmy heard the clatter of silverware against the china as they all started to eat. He could smell the syrup and the inviting fragrance of sausage, but somehow his fork wouldn't go into the hot cakes; perhaps they had been cooked too well, because they were very hard. He tried to cut them with his knife, but there was something wrong.

Jimmy left the hot cakes and found the sausage. He held it steady with his fork while he tried to cut off a bite with his knife. The knife went halfway through and stopped. He pushed a little harder with his knife and the sausage jumped off his plate like a tiddly-wink. Jimmy felt very much ashamed; he didn't know what to do. He sat very still for a moment and then he heard Mr. Weeks,

Nora, and Miss Young at the end of the dining room
giggling and trying not to laugh.

Mr. Weeks came back to the table. He had not gone
to the telephone at all. "Hold it, Mr. MacDonald!" He
put his hand on Mack's shoulder. "You can't eat that."

Jimmy realized that he wasn't the only one having
trouble with his food.

"You students know what the date is today?" Mr.
Weeks asked.

Nora and Miss Young called out together, "It's Hal-
loween! The goblins have been playing tricks on you."
Then they explained what they had done. The hot cakes
were layers of cardboard with a little syrup poured on
the top one, and Nora had pushed a skewer lengthwise
right through the middle of the sausage. Of course that
explained why they were having so much trouble eating.
Nora took the plates away, took the skewers out of the
sausage, and served everyone with delicious hot cakes.

The particular stunt that Mack had pulled was not on
the program. He had leaned forward, determined to cut
the cardboard hot cakes, and his necktie hung into his
plate. He picked up the end of the necktie with his fork
and brought it to his mouth; then, feeling something
dangling over his chin, he had tried to get that into his
mouth too — like a person eating spaghetti.

"If I hadn't stopped you, Mr. MacDonald, you would
have choked yourself with your own necktie," Mr. Weeks
told him.

"We didn't play this trick on you to be mean," Miss
Young explained, "but to show you the importance of
good table manners. Don't be embarrassed if something

goes wrong while you are eating. There's always a natural way to eat nicely."

Mr. Weeks took the students to the city that morning and taught them how to get on the bus with their dogs. He explained that guide dogs are allowed to ride on trains, airplanes, buses, and streetcars when accompanied by their blind masters.

The students got off the bus in a very crowded section of the city. Mr. Weeks wanted to teach them how to walk on busy streets, go through revolving doors, and ride in elevators with their dogs.

Jimmy waited for the signal at the street crossing, then gave Sirius the command "Forward." They had taken only a few steps when Jimmy was stopped by Sirius stepping in front of him. The dog pressed its ribs against Jimmy's shins, and with the weight of its body forced Jimmy to take a step backward.

At that instant Jimmy heard the screech of tires skidding and felt the rush of air as an automobile whizzed past in front of him, so close that the hub caps scraped against Sirius' fur. The car was making a right turn and coming too fast to stop. If Sirius had not forced Jimmy back a step, they both would have been in the path of the speeding car. Sirius had risked his own life to save Jimmy.

As soon as the car had passed, Sirius stepped back to Jimmy's side and led him safely across the street. Jimmy heard people shouting at the driver; many of them sounded very angry, but the driver just went on.

When they reached the sidewalk, Jimmy knelt down and put his arms around the dog. Sirius licked Jimmy's

face as if to say, "It's all in the day's work, and that's what I'm here for."

Jimmy rose from his knees and took hold of the harness.

"That's a good dog you've got there." A man's voice near him was speaking to Jimmy.

"He's wonderful," Jimmy answered. "He just saved my life."

"I saw it," the man told him. "Are they trained to do that?"

"I don't know, sir, but he sure takes care of me."

"Well, good luck, young fellow," the voice said.

"Thank you, sir," and Jimmy walked quickly down the sidewalk.

Sirius wove in and out among the people on the sidewalk. He would see an opening and make for it, judging the space so accurately that Jimmy never bumped into anyone. If a group was blocking the sidewalk, Sirius put his nose against the calf of a leg and pushed. Looking down, the person would see the large dog and step aside quickly, making a clear path.

Jimmy didn't know why he could walk down a crowded sidewalk and have so much room. One day Mr. Weeks told Jimmy what was happening. "Don't let your dog crowd through people, Mr. Carter," he added, "or you will become unpopular."

"How can I stop him?" Jimmy asked.

"I guess you'll have to teach him manners," Mr. Weeks answered.

"He's got manners, Mr. Weeks, but they're bad." Jimmy grinned.

"Then teach him good ones," Mr. Weeks said. "Hold your dog to a slower pace in a crowd," he added.

Jimmy occasionally heard remarks while walking with Sirius: "Isn't that beautiful?" or "Isn't that wonderful?"

Jimmy would smile to himself. He knew the people were not talking about him; they were talking about the dog.

"But someday," he promised himself, "I'll make them feel that way about me."

Chapter
TWELVE

ONE NIGHT at the end of the second week of training
Mack and Jimmy were in their room getting ready for
bed. The two dogs curled up in their separate corners.

"We're halfway through our course, Jim." Mack took
off his tie, folded it carefully, and laid it on the corner
of the dresser where he could find it.

"Oh, I'm not ready to go home," Jimmy said. "What
would I do without Mr. Weeks?" He saw himself and
Sirius lost a few blocks from home with no trainer to
send help.

"Wait a minute, Jim. Don't get discouraged," Mack
said. "Before you came here, would you have believed
you could walk ten or twelve blocks in a strange town all
by yourself?"

"No," Jimmy admitted. "I guess we have learned a lot,
but I'm not ready to graduate."

"None of us is," Mack said. "We've got two more
weeks to go, and I'm going to crawl into bed and get
ready for them."

Jimmy heard Smoky's toenails on the floor as he came
out of the corner to lie under Mack's bed. As Jimmy got
into bed, he heard Sirius come over to him. That's pretty

smart, he thought. The dogs get into a corner out of the way while we're walking about the room. He could hear Smoky settling down to sleep, making satisfied little noises, and Sirius' quiet breathing under his bed.

Jimmy lay there thinking what it would be like when he went home. He thought of the boys in his group.

"Mack!" he called quietly.

"Now what?"

"How can a blind person beat up a sighted guy?"

"Why should he want to?" Mack asked.

"I was thinking of Mike Adams, who threw the firecracker in my face and did this to me."

"He didn't do it on purpose, did he?"

"I don't know for sure, but he did it, and I've got to get even with him," said Jimmy.

"That won't help you, Jim. I felt that way about the fellow who hit me with his car. He wanted to visit me at the hospital."

"Mike never came to see me, and it's a good thing."

"You're wrong, Jim. You've got to quit hating him," Mack said seriously.

"Fat chance." Jimmy clenched his fist.

"I understand how you feel," Mack went on. "I hated the guy that hit me until his father came to see me."

"Yeah? What did he do?"

"He asked me the question that I'm going to ask you."

"What?"

"Just this. How would you like to go through life knowing you made someone else go blind?"

Jimmy was silent for a moment. "You mean Mike has that on his conscience and it worries him?"

"Certainly. In some ways he's worse off than you are," Mack answered. "I'll bet the guy that ran over me has never driven a car again."

"But I've got it on my conscience, too. I dream about him. The dream always ends with a flash of light and a loud crashing noise. Then I wake up trying to scream."

"That's because you still hate him, Jim, and you're troubled over it. If you could feel sorry for him, you'd get rid of your dream the way I did."

"Did you have dreams like that?"

"Sort of. I would see the car coming and try to jump out of the way, but it always swerved right at me and I would wake up trembling."

"But how did you get rid of that dream?" Jimmy asked.

"I let the driver talk to me and realized how he felt. I bet your Mike is having a hard time, too."

"The gang won't play with him, and it serves him right."

"No, Jim. There's no use in both of your lives' being ruined."

"I never thought of that," Jimmy said slowly. "What should I do?"

"Try to be friends with him, and I promise you'll never have that dream again," Mack said.

"I don't know if I can. I'll have to think about it," Jimmy answered. "Maybe we're both having a rough time."

"Both of you are. I'm sure of that."

"The fellows tell me that Mike has got mean, and he used to be a right guy."

"Sure, he's sore at the way the gang treats him and

sore at himself for what he did to you. It's up to you to clear it up."

"I don't know," Jimmy repeated slowly.

"Think about it, Jim," and Mack turned over to go to sleep.

Jimmy lay awake for quite a while, thinking.

The next two weeks passed quickly, and in spite of his fears Jimmy was ready to graduate with the rest of the class. Dressed in their best clothes, the students were assembled in the recreation room of the school with an audience of friends and relatives. The dogs also had been especially brushed and curried for the occasion. They were taken away from the students to be formally presented to them like diplomas.

A reception followed the simple but very impressive ceremony, and Jimmy met Judy Lane, a member of the local 4-H Club, who had raised Sirius. He thanked her for taking care of his dog.

"He was my dog first," Judy said, "and I had him longer than you."

Jimmy didn't like that. "How long did you have him?" he asked.

"Almost a year. He was just a puppy, and he was the cutest thing!"

Jimmy was getting a little jealous. "Well, he's not cute now. He's a swell dog."

"I know. He was trained for five months after they took him away from me." There was a wistful note in the girl's voice. She knelt down to hug the dog. Sirius licked her face and then went to stand in front of Jimmy.

"Don't you remember me, Sirius? I'm Judy." The girl

looked sadly at the dog. "Have you forgotten me already? I raised you."

Sirius flapped his ears, jingled his chain collar, and looked up at Jimmy.

"Don't be disappointed, Judy," Jimmy told her. "Sirius knows how badly I need him, and dogs want to be of service. I think he'd rather be my four-legged eyes than be just a pet, even for you."

"Of course," Judy said. "I'm going to get another puppy to raise as soon as they have one ready for me."

Jimmy's mother could not get away from her office to attend the graduation, so Miss Young made Jimmy's reservation for the plane trip home. Jimmy was sorry in a way to leave his new friends and the school where he had learned so much, but was anxious to get back home to show off his dog and let his friends see how well he could get along with his new eyes. He felt very grown-up and completely independent.

Mr. Weeks drove Jimmy out to the airport in the now familiar station wagon.

"This will be my first airplane ride, Mr. Weeks. I'm wondering how I'll feel about it." Jimmy was a little nervous.

"It's your dog's first trip too, and if you're nervous the dog will know it, so you'd better not be afraid."

"How can I help it if I am?" Jimmy asked.

Mr. Weeks laughed. "Pretend you're still on the ground. You won't see the difference."

The brakes squeaked as the station wagon came to a stop.

"Take my arm," Mr. Weeks said. "The dog can't lead

you unless you know where you're going. You'll have to muzzle him when you get on the plane."

"Muzzle him? Why? Sirius won't bite anybody." He grinned and added, "I mean Leader."

"You may call him Leader now if you wish," Mr. Weeks said. "As for the muzzle, the reason has nothing to do with the dog's being gentle. He must wear a muzzle when the plane takes off and when you land, and at all times when the passengers put on their safety belts. If any of the passengers got frightened, the dog would get excited and add to the confusion. It's just a matter of safety, like the safety belt. Here's your plane."

He introduced Jimmy to the hostess, then continued. "So long, Jimmy. I wish you a lot of luck and success. You and Sirius — I mean Leader — are going to get along fine."

The hostess led Jimmy and Leader to a seat, helped to adjust Jimmy's safety belt, and asked, "Is this your first flight?"

"Yes." Jimmy fingered the wide belt with its strange buckle.

"A sign lights up to tell the passengers when to fasten their safety belts," the hostess said. "I'll tell you when the light goes off and you can loosen your belt."

"Thank you," said Jimmy.

"May I sit next to you?" she asked. "I'd like to know about these dogs. I think they're wonderful."

"I'd like to tell you about Leader." Jimmy reached forward to pet the dog.

"I'll come back to you later," the hostess said. "Now I must check in the rest of my passengers."

Suddenly there was a roar and a vibration throughout the plane as the motors started. The dog stood up and thrust his muzzle into Jimmy's hand. "It's all right, Leader," Jimmy said, stroking the dog soothingly. When all four motors were idling evenly, the dog lay down again.

The plane taxied down the runway and headed into the wind. Jimmy felt the plane lurch forward and bump along the ground; then the bumping stopped and Jimmy realized they must be airborne. Leader was lying at Jimmy's feet as unimpressed as if he were on a car ride.

The hostess came to say that the light was out. Jimmy unbuckled his safety belt and took off Leader's muzzle.

"Here is a button that you can press when you want to call me." The hostess took Jimmy's fingers to place them on the button on the wall beside him. "And here above it is an air jet."

"What's that for?" Jimmy asked. "Isn't this a pressurized cabin?"

"Yes," she answered. "This is for cold fresh air if it gets too warm. Here, I'll show you. Feel this little nozzle? You can turn that in any direction you wish, and this wheel behind it turns on the air."

Jimmy turned it on and directed the little stream of air toward himself.

"It might be better if you turned this cool air toward your dog," the hostess suggested. "It must be warm on the floor between the seats."

"I'll do that," Jimmy said. "Okay, Leader, I'll turn on the oxygen. You won't need your space suit till we're ready to land."

The hostess laughed. "I'll have to check your ticket," she said. "If you're booked through to the moon you'll have to transfer at the outer-space landing field; we don't go through. Now here's something else." She showed Jimmy a button on the arm of his chair. "This adjusts the back of your seat so you can lean back. Sorry, but I'll have to leave you now. One of the other passengers is calling me."

Jimmy pressed the button and leaned so far back that he thought he was lying in the lap of the passenger behind him. He sat up and pressed the button again. The back sprang up and slapped him between the shoulders, almost knocking him out of the seat.

Immediately Leader was on his feet to see who had struck his master, trying to find out what was going on. He nuzzled at Jimmy's hand as if asking, "Well, what happened? Who hit you?"

Jimmy laughed and stroked the dog's head. "It's all right, Leader." Leader seemed satisfied. Putting his front paws on the seat he reached over to lick Jimmy's face, and then curled up contentedly on the floor.

Jimmy again pressed the button on the arm rest and shoved back gently to a comfortable position.

A little later on the trip he felt Leader get up, walk over toward the side of the plane and then come back to lie *on* Jimmy's feet, not *at* them. The man across the aisle laughed and leaned over to say, "I must tell you what your dog just did. He walked over and put his paws on the side of the plane to look out the window. Then his ears went flat down against his head, his tail tight between his legs, and he came back to lie on your feet."

"I wondered why he did that," Jimmy said.

"He didn't like what he saw out there," the man answered. "Too much empty space — just too much of
nothing."

Now Jimmy realized that he was high in the air. Not
being able to see through the window, he felt as if he
were in a bus or an automobile. He wasn't a bit nervous,
and so Leader was not afraid either when he lay at
Jimmy's feet.

After a while the hostess came to his side. "Will you
fasten your safety belt now, please?"

"Why?" Jimmy asked. "Is anything wrong?"

"Oh no," the hostess told him. "We'll be coming in to
a landing in a few minutes."

"Landing? You mean we're home already?"

"Yes, it doesn't take long on a plane. If you'll wait until
I take care of my passengers, I'll come back and help
you."

"Thank you," Jimmy said. Then, after a pause, "Could
you tell me something?" He waited, but there was no
answer. "I guess she's gone," he told himself. "Well, I'll
have to put the muzzle on Leader."

He had to loosen his safety belt to get the muzzle out
of his coat pocket, and he left the belt loose while he
leaned forward to put the muzzle on the dog. Leader was
not very much help. He shook his head and backed up to
get his nose out of the muzzle.

Jimmy didn't know what to do. He didn't want to
scold Leader, and he didn't want to get in trouble by not
having the muzzle on when it should be. He was just
about ready to give up and call the hostess for help when

Leader gave up and let Jimmy put on the muzzle, as if to say, "I don't like the old thing, but if I have to wear it I'll just put up with it."

Jimmy tightened his safety belt and sat waiting for the plane to land. What would he do after it landed? How would he get to the waiting room? Mr. Weeks had brought him to the plane, but who would take him from it? "Leader, I guess you're elected." The dog's ears went up, and he looked at Jimmy as if waiting for orders.

"How are we going to get to the waiting room, Leader?" He leaned forward to scratch the dog's head. "Can you take me? You see, I don't know where it is, so I can't tell you. Mr. Weeks didn't tell me what to do about that. Maybe he told you, Leader, when I wasn't listening."

Jimmy was getting nervous. Suppose his mother were not there to meet him! Suppose she had not got the telegram! And if she was there, how would he find her?

Leader seemed to feel that something was wrong and rubbed the side of his face against Jimmy's hands, but that didn't solve the problem. Then Jimmy noticed the hum of the motors change; they were not so high-pitched now. He thought it might be his ears; they felt strange. He swallowed and everything sounded different. "Hey, my ears popped! Leader, did your ears pop?"

Jimmy felt a very slight bump and the motors dropped to idling. "We must be on the ground, Leader. We've landed. We've had our first airplane ride." He tried to imagine what the plane was doing. He thought it went down the runway and it seemed to turn around and taxi back. Then it stopped.

The people on the plane were talking and getting ready to get off. "Just keep your seat and I'll be right back for you." The hostess was at his shoulder and then gone again.

Jimmy released his safety belt and sat waiting. "Now I'll take you to the administration building." It was the hostess again.

"Will you help me find my mother?" Jimmy asked.

"Oh, is your mother meeting you? She'll probably come out to the plane. Here, come along with me." She guided him along the aisle and down the ramp to the ground.

Chapter
THIRTEEN

Jimmy, here I am!" Jimmy heard his mother's voice calling.

Leader stiffened with a little growl of warning. He didn't know this strange woman rushing at them. He wasn't sure that it was all right. "Mom," called Jimmy. "Where are you?" And Leader relaxed at the cheerful tone in Jimmy's voice.

Jimmy was gathered into his mother's arms. "Why, Jimmy, you've grown in just a month. You look fine."

The hostess stepped back as she smiled at Mrs. Carter. "Well, good-by, Jimmy. It was nice having you with me."

"Thanks," Jimmy said to her, and then to his mother, "Mom, this was my hostess on the plane."

"Thank you for taking care of Jimmy," Mrs. Carter said. "I hope he was no trouble."

"Not a bit," the hostess assured her. "He was a perfect passenger, and so was the dog." She turned and left them.

Mrs. Carter looked down. "Oh, is this the dog?"

"Yes, Mom, isn't he swell?" Jimmy dropped to one knee with his arm around the dog's neck. "His name is Leader, Mom, and he's just wonderful."

"Yes, he's beautiful." Mrs. Carter reached toward the dog slowly. He was still a strange dog and very large. She wasn't quite sure.

"He'll shake hands, Mom, if you say 'Howdy do' like this: 'Howdy do, Leader.' See, Mom, see! Oh, I guess I can take the muzzle off now."

Mrs. Carter thought she would be just as well pleased if he left it on for a while, but she didn't say anything.

Jimmy unbuckled the muzzle, and Leader shook his head, flapping his ears and rattling his chain collar. "Now Mom, shake hands with him. You'll have to stoop down."

"When we get home we can get to know each other, Jimmy. Where's your baggage check?"

"I've got it in my inside pocket with my ticket stub." He felt very important, like a world traveler returning home. After the baggage was unloaded from the plane, they claimed the suitcase and Mrs. Carter called a taxi. "What do we do with the dog?" she asked. "Where do we put him?"

"He goes right along with us, Mom. Just like in the station wagon."

As Mrs. Carter led Jimmy to the taxi, he tried to remember what Mr. Weeks had taught him about entering a bus. Leader hung back until Jimmy got into the cab, then piled in after him. Mrs. Carter squeezed over in a corner of the seat.

"Mom," Jimmy said when they got started, "that Braille slate you gave me was swell. Could Carolyn read the letters I wrote on it?"

"Yes, Jimmy. She did very well. Of course she had a lot of time to study them out."

"What do you mean, Mom, 'a lot of time'?"

"Well, you didn't write to us very often, so she had time to puzzle out what you said in one letter before we got the next one."

"I did so. I wrote lots of times, only you answered so quick I couldn't keep up with 'em."

"I was only teasing, Jimmy." Mrs. Carter gave him a quick hug. "I think you did very well. Who read my letters to you?"

"Miss Young, the social worker. She taught me how to eat by myself, and you've got to mark my clothes and — oh, lots of things."

As they were driven home Jimmy tried to tell his mother everything that had happened during the past month, and she interrupted with many questions.

When they arrived home, Jimmy took off Leader's harness and let him run and sniff about the house. The dog ran into every room, sniffing in every corner.

"What's the matter with him, Jimmy? Is he all right?" his mother asked. "Why is he doing that?"

"Oh, he's just getting acquainted, Mom. He's got to find out if he likes this place."

Leader ran into Jimmy's room and stood with his head cocked on one side. He seemed to recognize that this was Jimmy's room. It was much like the room at school. He appeared to be satisfied and came back with tail wagging, to lie at Jimmy's feet. Mrs. Carter looked down at the dog and said, as if to herself, "He can sleep on the porch until we get a house built for him."

"House for him! On the porch! You mean Leader, Mom?"

"Why yes, Jimmy. He'll have to sleep somewhere."

"But he stays with me, Mom. He wouldn't be happy if we were separated." Jimmy was getting worried.

"You won't be separated, but he's such a large dog. We wouldn't have any furniture left."

"You don't understand, Mom. He sleeps under my bed."

"But Jimmy, that dog could never get under your bed. You know it isn't high enough."

"Gee, I never thought of that!" He paused, then grinned. "Guess they should have given me a dachshund."

"I guess they should have given you a pony stable," his mother corrected.

"He'll be all right in my room. You'll see, Mom. Just like in school."

Leader looked from one face to the other as if he too were waiting for Mrs. Carter's decision.

"Well, we'll try it out," his mother decided. "I'll fold an old blanket on the floor. Perhaps he can sleep on that."

"Thanks, Mom. That'll be keen." Jimmy laid his hand on the dog to tell him that everything was all right.

"What about food and water, Jimmy?" Mrs. Carter asked.

"Gee, I forgot," said Jimmy. "I guess we'll have to get over to the market."

"Can't you use the box of food Chuck and Art gave you?"

"Sure," said Jimmy. "I guess so. Can I keep a pan of water in the kitchen? He won't mess up the floor."

Mrs. Carter may have had her doubts about that, but she gave permission just the same.

"Let's see if he's thirsty now. What pan can I have?"

The three of them went to the kitchen, where Mrs. Carter selected a pan and filled it with water.

"Wait, Mom. I've got to take care of him. No one else can feed him. That's a rule."

"Then you give him the water." Mrs. Carter watched as he carried the pan of water over to a corner and set it down without spilling it.

"Here, Leader, want some water?" The dog looked at the dish and then looked up at Jimmy. That was not his water dish, and he hesitated. "Okay, Leader." Jimmy knelt beside the dish and pointed to it. "Come, Leader. Have some water."

The dog went over to it, lapped a couple of times to see if it was all right, looked at Jimmy, and then drank thirstily.

"I'll have to have another dish for his food. Will it be all right, Mom?"

"Why certainly, Jimmy. Get the box off the table in your room while I get a dish."

Jimmy started out, and immediately Leader was at his heels. They returned, with Leader scampering about, very much interested in the box of food. "As soon as he's fed, Mom, I want to show you how he works."

Jimmy measured out the food, and they both stood and watched Leader eat. Then they went to the living room, where Jimmy put the harness and leash on the dog. "If you'll stand on the front porch, Mom, I've got to teach Leader that this is home."

Mrs. Carter was not quite sure she understood, but Jimmy seemed to know so well what he was doing. "Tell me what you want me to do," she said. She followed as Jimmy and Leader went out the front door and crossed the porch.

Leader led Jimmy to the edge of the steps. His mother was about to call to him, but checked herself just in time as she saw Leader stop and Jimmy reach out with his foot to find the steps. "Now, Mom, you stay here and call to me when I'm right in front of the gate on my way back," Jimmy said.

"Where are you going?" she asked, a little troubled.

"You'll see. Just call when I'm in front of the gate."

She watched in amazement as Leader led Jimmy down the steps, along the path to the sidewalk, and halfway up the block, walking quickly; then she saw them turn around and come back. "Here, Jimmy," she called as they got in front of the gate.

"Left! Inside, Leader. Home, Leader, home!" she heard Jimmy command, and the dog turned left, came inside, and stopped at the foot of the stairs.

"Jimmy, that's wonderful."

"Now I must do this again, Mom, going in the opposite direction." They repeated the performance, going half a block to the left.

Again his mother called to them as they returned in front of the gate. She watched the dog bring Jimmy up the steps and into the house as carefully as she herself could have led him.

"Now Leader knows this is home, Mom, and he'll turn in of his own accord," Jimmy said proudly.

Impulsively Mrs. Carter stretched out her hands to the dog. "You wonderful dog!"

Leader looked up at Jimmy and then went straight into Mrs. Carter's arms. She hugged him and he licked her face as much as to say, "I understand. We both love him, and we'll take care of him."

She looked at the dog as if in agreement and said softly under her breath, "You are a wonderful dog, but will you be able to help Jimmy achieve a normal life?"

Chapter

FOURTEEN

THAT AFTERNOON Jimmy was in his room resting, with Leader lying by his bed, when Carolyn came home from school. "Is he home, Mom?" she called. "Did he bring the dog?" Before Mrs. Carter could answer, Carolyn threw her books to one side and rushed toward Jimmy's room.

"Hi, Midget!" Jimmy scrambled to his feet to go toward her.

Carolyn stopped short in the doorway. Leader was standing in the middle of the room, his head cocked to one side, his ears up, and the hackles on the back of his neck raised just a little. He was not belligerent. He was strictly defensive. A strange girl had rushed toward the room, and he was not going to let her in until he saw how his master felt about it. He gave one low growl of warning and stood like a statue, watching her.

Carolyn stepped back, surprised and a little disappointed. She had wanted to love the dog, but it looked as if he were not going to let her. Before she could decide what she really thought, Jimmy grabbed her by both shoulders and shook her. "Hi, Midget! Come and meet my new eyes. Come, Leader!"

Now Leader was satisfied that the strange girl was all right, and he was all dog. He came toward them, his tail wagging a greeting; and when Carolyn knelt down to hug him, he accepted the caress.

"Oh, Jimmy, he's a darling, but he's bigger than I thought," she said. "What did you say his name was?"

"I changed his name to Leader." At the sound of his name, Leader left her embrace and went over to Jimmy.

"Tell me all about him," Carolyn said. "What does he do and how does he work? Where's he gonna sleep?"

"Wait a minute! One at a time," Jimmy told her. He went back to sit on the bed.

"I think you've grown since you've been away," Carolyn said.

"I ought to," Jimmy answered. "I've been working like a horse and eating like a team."

Leader walked over to the side of the room and lay down where he could watch both of them.

"What was it all like?" Carolyn asked.

"Look, Midget, we've got a whole year for me to tell you about it. Don't expect me to put a whole month in a few minutes. Where's Art and Chuck?"

"Oh!" Carolyn jumped up. "I promised to phone them as soon as you came home. If I get them over here you'll talk plenty, and I can listen in." She ran out to the phone and Jimmy lay back across the bed.

He heard snatches of the one-sided conversation as she talked to Chuck and then repeated it to Art. He smiled as he listened. Somehow he felt very sure of himself. Again he was the big brother, not dependent upon Carolyn's help.

He sat up and reached out his hand. Instantly Leader came over and licked it to tell Jimmy he was there. "Good boy, Leader. With you to help me I can do things again."

Carolyn rushed back to the room, and Leader swung around quickly with a low sharp bark of warning. "Quiet, Leader. What's the matter with you?" Jimmy asked.

Leader came to him with his ears down, trying to apologize. "Midget," Jimmy said, "you must never rush in on the dog. It's all right, Leader." He interrupted himself to pat the dog and then went on. "You came at us suddenly, and Leader was frightened. He's all right now. Come over and make up with him; or better yet, stay where you are and call him."

Carolyn wasn't sure she wanted to call him, or that Leader wanted to come to her, but she stretched out her hand and called him gently. Leader came to her, his tail wagging happily. "Jimmy," Carolyn said, as she smoothed the hair on Leader's head, "he's got a black streak between his ears running down the center of his head. It looks as if his hair were parted in the middle."

"Yeah." Jimmy laughed. "I part it for him every morning with a currycomb."

Leader looked up and licked Carolyn's cheek. They had forgiven each other, accepted each other, and formed a lasting friendship.

Chuck and Art hurried through their home chores that afternoon, thinking more of Jimmy and the dog than they did of their work. As soon as they were excused from their dinner tables that night, both of them rushed over to the Carter home, getting there about the same time.

Carolyn had guessed right. She sat back and listened while the boys all talked at once. They asked new questions before Jimmy could answer the last ones.

"He sure is a good-looking dog, Jimmy." Chuck was studying the dog. "I guess you know what he looks like."

"No," Jimmy answered, "not really. They tried to tell me at the school, but everyone called the colors by different names."

"I wish you could see him." Art looked at Jimmy's face, then at the dog. "He's marked exactly the same on both sides. I mean, he's even, without splotches where they don't belong."

"Tell me," Jimmy said. "I think he's black with a fawn-colored underbody and legs. His haunches are fawn, blending into the black. Am I right?"

"Yes, but his head is marked like somebody painted it," Chuck said. "There's a tan patch on top of his head between the ears, with a black streak running down the center."

"I said his hair was parted in the middle," Carolyn giggled.

The boys laughed. "It does look sort of like that. See if you can get this, Jimmy," Chuck went on. "His ruff is tan, shading into a light gray on his chest and shirt front."

"And a black velvet nose and gorgeous brown eyes," Carolyn added.

"He sure is good-looking," Art said.

Leader was curled up at Jimmy's feet with his head cocked on one side, looking from one to the other as they spoke, as if checking up on the description, but soon he seemed to lose interest. He put his nose down between his paws with an indifference that almost said, "What I look like isn't so important. You ought to see what I *do!*" And he heaved a little sigh of contentment.

"Say, what's going on in school?" Jimmy asked. "You fellows are way ahead of me."

"You just missed September, October, and part of this month," Chuck said. "You can catch up."

"But starting in junior high — the work may be different and too hard for me." Jimmy shook his head. "Well, maybe I can if you both help me. And say," he added, "Leader says thanks for the dog biscuits. He ate some this afternoon."

Chuck quickly reached into his coat pocket and drew out a card. Looking at it, he said, "One, three, five, seven. One, three, nine. Two, five, six."

"Hey, that's keen," Jimmy said. "That's swell, Chuck!"

"Wait a minute, you went too fast!" Art complained. "I got lost. What's two, five, six?"

"It's the period," Chuck and Jimmy said together.

"What on earth!" Carolyn looked from one to the other, her head on one side, a pucker between her eyebrows.

"Didn't you get it, Midget? Didn't you understand?"

"Sounded crazy." Carolyn still studied their faces. "What is it — Scout talk?" Then she brightened. "Oh, I get it. Football signals, huh?"

"Nope!" Jimmy said loftily. "Just man talk. Women wouldn't know about these things."

"Humph!" Carolyn said. "I never knew Art was a woman. He didn't know!"

The boys laughed and talked on in their Braille code until Mrs. Carter, afraid Jimmy would be overtired, suggested they call it a day.

The next morning, after Carolyn had gone to school and Mrs. Carter to the office, Jimmy harnessed Leader and walked up and down the block in front of the house; occasionally they went inside to remind Leader where they lived. Then he went around the block, as he had with his white cane, only this time there was no need to watch for landmarks, no need to feel his way cautiously along. He and Leader went to the corner, walking faster than most people do, turned right, and before he knew it they were around the block and back home. They took their exercise that day going around the block like a pony on a merry-go-round. Jimmy didn't know that he had an audience, but many of the neighbors were watching with smiles of encouragement.

A few days later Jimmy dressed with extra care. He was going with his mother to see the school superintendent to arrange to go back to school.

"You almost look very nice," his mother said as he sat across from her at the breakfast table.

"Almost?" Jimmy wondered what he had done or forgotten to do. He knew he had put on a fresh shirt and his good trousers. He raised his hand to his hair. That was it — he had forgotten all about combing his hair. He had stood in front of the mirror when he brushed his teeth, but the mirror had told him nothing.

"We will have to get a new looking glass, Mom," he said, grinning. His mother looked up sharply. "You didn't break the glass!"

"Oh no, it isn't broken."

"Then why do we need a new one?" she asked.

"This one can't talk. It didn't tell me my hair wasn't combed."

"That's no excuse, young man," his mother scolded. "You know you have to think of things like that."

After breakfast, Jimmy, his mother, and Leader went to the school superintendent's office. Arrangements were made for Jimmy to learn typing. He would do his lessons in Braille and then type them to hand in to his teacher. A home teacher would help him to learn to do arithmetic in Braille. He would not need the student reader often supplied for the blind, since Chuck, Art, or Carolyn could read his lessons to him.

Everything seemed all right until the superintendent remarked, "You know you can't take the dog to school."

Jimmy didn't know anything of the sort. "We can't be separated. He's my eyes."

"Junior-college or college students may have their guide dogs," the superintendent explained, "but it would cause too much confusion in the lower grades. Some of the children might tease him and make him bite."

Jimmy's chin didn't quiver this time. He did not start to cry. He just refused to go to school if Leader couldn't go along. There was nothing anyone could do about it. The rules could not be changed, and the law required that Jimmy go to school.

"You might go to the State School for the Blind," the superintendent suggested, "but I'm quite sure that the dog could not go with you even there."

"I don't want to go to a blind school. I'm not blind when I have Leader. He's my four-legged eyeglasses."

"But you still can't take him to school," the superintendent told him patiently.

"There are a lot of people who have to wear glasses,"

Jimmy argued, "and they can't see when they take them off. You wouldn't make them leave their glasses at home."

"It's not quite the same," the superintendent explained. "You can't put your dog in your pocket."

Mrs. Carter decided to go home and think about it. She phoned Aunt Martha to discuss the problem with her.

"Why don't you phone that nice welfare worker?" Aunt Martha suggested.

"That's a good idea," Mrs. Carter said. "I'll call Miss Thompson, but she can't change the law. Jimmy must go to school, and he can't take the dog."

"Maybe I'm asking for trouble," Aunt Martha said, "and it might not work out at that."

"Don't talk in riddles, Martha. What do you mean?"

"I thought Jimmy might leave his dog with me while he is at school," Aunt Martha explained. "He has to pass right by here, now that he is starting at junior high."

"That would be fine, Martha, but I don't know if I can make Jimmy do it."

"And I don't know if the dog would stay with me," Aunt Martha added.

"Well, it's the best suggestion I've had so far," Mrs. Carter said wearily.

"I'll probably regret it," Aunt Martha told her. "Call me back after you've spoken to Miss Thompson."

"I'll come right out," Miss Thompson agreed when Mrs. Carter phoned her. "I haven't seen the new dog."

When Miss Thompson arrived, Mrs. Carter told her of Aunt Martha's suggestion, and again Jimmy vetoed the entire idea.

"Leader is your guide," Miss Thompson said, "and you need him, but you must protect him as he protects you."

"What do you mean?" Jimmy asked. "Sure I protect him."

"The dog would be very uncomfortable, cramped under a desk all day, and would be in the way if he were in the aisle. You really don't need him indoors any more than you did your white cane."

It all made sense, but Jimmy didn't like it. "Leader wouldn't stay with Aunt Martha," he complained.

"He wouldn't like it any more than you do," Miss Thompson admitted, "but it is the only answer. Let Leader take you to your aunt, and then you can go the short distance to the school with your white cane. Get Leader again after school and he can take you wherever you want to go."

"It's the only way we can work it out, Jimmy," his mother explained. "None of us likes it."

"I can't go back to a white cane." Jimmy reached over to pet Leader. "That's making me go blind all over again." He knelt to hug the dog. "We were just beginning to get along so well. I won't give him up, that's all. I just won't."

"You're not giving him up, Jimmy," Miss Thompson said. "You're doing what's best for the dog."

After much argument, Jimmy agreed to try it out for one day to see if it would work. "Leader will just tear the house down if I go away and leave him. He'll wreck everything in the place."

"Let's try the trip while I'm with you," Miss Thompson suggested. "We'll stop at your aunt's; then I'll go with you to be sure you know your way about the school."

"Good thing it's after school. There won't be a bunch of kids around," Jimmy grumbled.

"Yes," Miss Thompson agreed, "it will be easier without the children. I'll carry your white cane until we get to your aunt's."

Jimmy started with confidence. He didn't need the trainer to lay out the route. He swung along beside Leader, with Miss Thompson hurrying to keep up with them. She admired the way the dog worked with the boy.

Aunt Martha was surprised when they arrived so quickly. Jimmy's mother had just called to tell her that they were on the way.

Aunt Martha understood dogs, and made friends with Leader. They played together while Miss Thompson quietly took Jimmy to the front door.

Jimmy started down the steps with his white cane, hurrying away from the house before Leader should notice that he was gone. They went down the block, across the side street and along the front of the school. Jimmy wasn't sure where to find the wide path leading to the front entrance.

Jimmy was not sure of a great many things. "If this was my old school I could get around better. I don't know what this place is like."

"Come along and we'll go exploring," Miss Thompson said.

The janitor met them in the main hall, and Miss Thompson explained their visit. He joined them, and together they "Brailled" the building until Jimmy was able to go without difficulty from one room to another and from the street back to his classroom.

"There are just too many things in the world, Miss Thompson," Jimmy complained.

"What sort of things, Jimmy?"

"No special sort. Just things. This table in the hall, and that flight of stairs coming down in the way."

"But you know where they are and can avoid them," Miss Thompson reminded him.

"And that jog where the hall gets narrower," Jimmy continued. "It's a long hall, Miss Thompson, and with this old white cane again I feel as if I'm going down a long dark corridor."

"It won't seem so long when this hall gets full of children, and there'll be a lot more to look out for," the janitor warned.

"Yeah," said Jimmy, "and I won't have Leader to guide me around them."

"You'll get along all right after the first few days," Miss Thompson said encouragingly.

"All the youngsters will help him," the janitor agreed.

"Maybe," Jimmy admitted. "Now can I go back to Leader?"

"Yes," Miss Thompson answered. "We will leave the white cane with your aunt and get the dog."

When Aunt Martha opened the door for them, Leader rushed at Jimmy as if he were going to eat him up. He jumped around in front of him, panting with excitement. Then, standing on his hind legs, he put his front paws on Jimmy's shoulders. Jimmy put an arm around the dog and drew him close, and Leader licked his face all the while.

Aunt Martha laughed. "Are you going to dance?"

Leader sat down in front of Jimmy, studying him, then reached over and licked Jimmy's hand.

"Yes, Leader," Miss Thompson said. "Count his fingers, but I'm sure they are all there." And Leader licked each one as if that were exactly what he was trying to do.

"Was he all right, Aunt Martha?" Jimmy asked anxiously.

Miss Thompson looked at Aunt Martha with a warning finger on her lips while she nodded her head.

Aunt Martha smiled. "Oh yes, he was fine! I'm the wreck."

Jimmy put the harness on Leader, who behaved as if he couldn't get out of the house fast enough. But after they reached the sidewalk, Leader settled down to his usual perfect job of guiding.

When they got home, Miss Thompson reported to Mrs. Carter that she believed the system would work out. Then she hesitated. "Now if we could only find some games or sports in which Jimmy would compete with the other boys."

Mrs. Carter smiled as she looked at the boy, standing straight and resolute beside his dog. "Jimmy will probably work that out for himself," she said quietly.

Chapter
FIFTEEN

THE FOLLOWING MONDAY MORNING Jimmy started bravely
for school. He swung along beside Leader with the dog
obeying his every command — that is, until they reached
the block where Aunt Martha lived. As they approached
her house, Leader gradually slowed his pace.

"Hop up, Leader — come on, let's go," Jimmy said, but
Leader didn't "hop up." He slowed down until they were
nearly in front of Aunt Martha's house, then came to life,
walking faster and faster, pulling Jimmy along with him.
When they were past the house, he slowed down to his
usual gait.

"Left, Leader, left! Inside," Jimmy commanded. The
dog must have heard the command, but showed no inten-
tion of obeying it. Jimmy repeated the command. "Left,
Leader, inside!" Then Leader turned and started to lead
Jimmy up the steps of a strange house.

Now Jimmy was confused. He wondered whether he
had gone too far or not far enough. Aunt Martha had
been watching, and when she saw them pass she came
to the door and called to them.

Jimmy started back. This time Leader had no excuse,
and when Jimmy gave the command he turned in slowly,

as if he did not like that house where Jimmy had gone away and left him.

Jimmy got his white cane, and after a very serious argument with Leader, and with Aunt Martha's help, he was able to get away. He had no trouble finding the school, guided by the noise of the children at play, but as he passed each group he noticed that they became strangely silent. He knew they were watching him, and wished he had Leader to show them how well he could get along. All right, he would show them anyhow. This was just another obstacle course.

He tried to see the school as Miss Thompson had shown it to him and to remember how they reached his classroom. He was so busy finding his way that he forgot all about the children who might be watching. The teacher came to him, and together they worked out a system to help Jimmy find his desk. Then Chuck and Art came into the room, and Jimmy's troubles seemed to be over.

At first the rest of the children seemed shy of Jimmy. They did not know just what to do, but when they saw how Art and Chuck treated him they tried to behave the same way.

When school was over for the day, Jimmy left, walking between Chuck and Art. The children had heard that Jimmy had a dog and were waiting to see it. They formed into groups and watched.

Later Jimmy learned that Mike Adams was at the edge of one of the groups, but Art and Chuck paid no attention to him. Mike watched the two boys, walking beside Jimmy as if they were proud to be there. He lowered his head and mumbled, "I didn't do it on purpose. It's not fair for them to blame me." He turned, roughly pushed a smaller boy out of his path, and elbowed his way out of the group.

Chuck and Art led Jimmy toward Aunt Martha's house, talking in their secret code.

"Hey!" called one of the group. "Listen how they're talking. That must be blind language."

"Sure," Chuck called back. "That's the way he talks to his dog — it's a German shepherd."

"Yeah?" The boy wasn't sure whether Chuck was joking or not.

Jimmy went into the house for his dog, as Chuck and Art went their separate ways. A few of the children remained, and when Jimmy came out with Leader he heard their excited voices. The children watched Jimmy and Leader walk down the street and turn the corner.

Mike also had followed Jimmy. He walked along behind him, watching Jimmy and his good-looking dog. He quickened his pace and came alongside, reaching out his hand to pet the dog. His hand swung out quickly to brush along the dog's back in a friendly gesture.

When Leader saw the hand swinging toward him, he drew protectingly closer to Jimmy, turned his head toward Mike, bared his teeth, and growled low in his throat.

Mike checked his friendly advance and stepped back in fear.

"Steady, Leader, steady!" Jimmy commanded. He wondered what had made Leader behave like that.

Leader settled down to his job, but jerked his head

around occasionally, looking behind him, ears up, his body tense and alert.

"Okay, Leader." Jimmy said to the dog. "I suppose there's a kitten in that front yard. Let it alone. It hasn't bothered us." As they walked on, Jimmy thought he heard a voice mumble. It sounded like, "I only wanted to pet the old dog," and he wondered what it was all about.

After that first meeting Leader was on guard against Mike, alert for another quick movement of Mike's hand. They often passed each other on the street; Mike would make some playful motion each time, teasing the dog, and Leader did not like it. It became a sort of game with Mike. Jimmy would scold the dog and walk on, wondering what made Leader restless.

He decided to ask Chuck or Art if they had noticed anything in the neighborhood that would make Leader behave that way — perhaps a stray dog or cat — but Jimmy forgot about it when they were together studying.

Chuck and Art studied with Jimmy after school, helping him to catch up with the rest of the class. They took turns reading aloud while Jimmy made notes in Braille, and the three of them would get into discussions, arguing about the subject they were studying.

"You know, Chuck," Art said one afternoon, "this science book makes more sense to me than it ever did before."

"Yeah," said Chuck, "I was just thinking, I'm learning this stuff myself."

Through their eyes, Jimmy studied a health book. It described the inside of the body and told stories of how people react to certain things. During the discussion of one of these stories, Mike Adams' name came up.

"I wonder if that's why Mike acts the way he does," Art said.

"Sure," Chuck said. "The book explains that. He thinks we're punishing him, so he's sore at us."

"Then he hasn't learned his lesson," Art insisted. "Take that boy they sent to Juvenile Hall in the book. He was a right guy when he came out."

"Maybe Mike ought to be sent to Juvenile Hall," Chuck suggested.

"No, you're wrong, both of you," Jimmy told them. "I felt that way until I talked with Mack, my roommate at the guide-dog school. We've got to give Mike another chance."

"Oh yeah?" Art said. "I think he's done enough."

"And he keeps on doing more," Chuck added.

"That's it," Jimmy said. "We're making him act that way. I understand it now. I'd like to talk to him."

"Are you crazy?" Art asked. "You want to tangle with Mike? Well, I guess Leader could protect you."

"Come on." Chuck picked up a book. "This isn't studying."

"It is, in a way," Jimmy answered, "but let's get on with the lesson. I've got to catch up to you fellows."

"There's something else I was thinking." Chuck closed the book on his finger. "You were class president last year. Are you going to run again?"

"I don't know," Jimmy said. "I — I don't think so."

"Why not?" Chuck looked at him. "The kids thought you were pretty good."

"That was last year," Jimmy reminded him. "It might be different now."

Chuck glanced at Art. "You mean because you're blind?"

"If that's it," Art put in, "heck, you could still do just as good a job."

"What I meant," Jimmy explained, "they might vote for me because they were sorry for me."

"Huh! Not that bunch," Chuck snorted. "They're not sorry for anything unless they get punished for it; and anyway" — he studied Jimmy's face — "they're getting to feel like us. You know, Jimmy, half the time I forget you can't see."

"That's funny." Jimmy grinned. "I forget it sometimes myself since I have Leader." He reached down to pet the dog.

The boys studied on until Mrs. Carter came in to remind them that it was almost dinnertime. Somehow the time always seemed to pass more quickly with the three of them studying together. Chuck and Art went home, and Jimmy washed up for dinner.

That evening Jimmy was drying the dishes as Carolyn washed them, when Mrs. Carter came into the kitchen.

"Mom!" Jimmy turned toward her.

"Yes, Jimmy."

"I'll be having some extra expenses soon, and I was thinking —"

"Look out, Mommy," Carolyn interrupted, "that sounds like the beginning of a touch."

"Nothing of the sort," Jimmy protested. "It's just the opposite. I've been thinking of earning some money."

"That would be fine, Jimmy," Mrs. Carter said. "What did you have in mind?"

Carolyn turned around, a plate in one hand, a dishcloth in the other. She looked at Jimmy as if he had said something in Chinese.

"One of the boys at the guide-dog school has a corner, and I believe I can get one."

Carolyn laid down the plate as if afraid she might drop it. "You sure you feel all right, Jimmy? What's wrong with him, Mommy?"

Mrs. Carter laughed. "Is that dog Latin, Jimmy? If so, I don't understand it."

"I'm not fooling," Jimmy went on. "He has a newspaper corner, and I bet I can get one and sell papers like he does."

"Oh, papers!" Carolyn turned back to her dishpan.

"Wouldn't that be dangerous?" his mother asked.

"Heck, no!" said Jimmy. "I wouldn't go into the street. People walking by would be okay, and the cars would have to drive up to the curb. You know, 'curb service only.' "

"You might begin that way," his mother said, "then get careless and go into the street to a car."

"No, Mom. Frank didn't do that. He's the boy at school, and he makes out okay."

"Well, we'll think about it," Mrs. Carter said. "I'm not sure I like it, but Jimmy" — she walked over to hug him — I'm proud of you for wanting to do it."

"I've just got to do it," Jimmy argued. "I — I want to go back into the Scouts." He paused and then went on as if thinking aloud. "Everything I do is interesting, but it isn't like playing outdoors with the rest of the fellows."

"I'd like you to go back to your Scouting, Jimmy." Then she hesitated. "If — if you can do it."

Jimmy ignored his mother's doubt. "I'll need a new sleeping bag and other equipment."

"We can probably take care of all that," his mother told him.

"But I want to earn my own equipment," Jimmy insisted. "Please, Mom."

"Let me think about it," she said. "I'll talk to Miss Thompson and perhaps a few other people. I promise, Jimmy, I'll think about it."

Mrs. Carter got a great deal of advice. Each person gave her a different answer and a different reason. Miss Thompson liked the idea, provided Jimmy would be careful, and she believed that he would.

Jimmy was not sure that he could get a corner, and decided to find out for himself. One afternoon after school he put on his good suit and, after getting complete directions, started out with Leader for the newspaper office. It was like being back at the guide-dog school, going into new territory and traveling an unfamiliar route. He thought he should be at the newspaper office when he heard a man's footsteps coming toward him on the sidewalk.

"Please, sir," he called out. "Is this the newspaper office?"

The footsteps paused. "Why, yes," the man said. "Did you want something?"

"Yes, sir. I want to find out where they sell the newspapers."

"Come along. I'll show you." The man took Jimmy's arm.

"The dog will take me if you show me the door."

"That's all right. I was going in anyway." The man opened the door for Jimmy and his dog. "Do you want to buy today's paper?"

"No, sir. I don't want to buy anything. I want to sell papers."

The man stopped. "But you couldn't handle a route."

"Not a route," Jimmy said. "I want a corner. I want to see if they will let me have one."

"Do you think you could handle a corner?" the man asked.

"Sure, if they'll let me." Jimmy squared his shoulders.

"But you don't see, do you?" the man asked kindly.

"That doesn't matter. I can do it if they'll let me try."

"And I believe you could." The man put his hand on Jimmy's shoulder.

"Whom do I have to see?" Jimmy asked. "I've got to sell him the idea."

"What's your name?" the man inquired. "I think you've already sold him the idea."

"I'm Jimmy Carter, sir. Will you please show me where I ought to go?"

"I'm Donald Blackburn. I'm business manager of the *Journal*, and I'll see to it that you get a corner."

"You, the manager? Gee!"

"Come along to the circulation department." He took Jimmy's arm. "I think we'll start you fairly light. You won't mind that, will you?"

"I'm not sure I know what that means."

"A corner not very busy to begin with. But look here, young man." He stopped and turned toward Jimmy. "You're to give me your solemn promise that you will not go into the street or step off the sidewalk. By the way, are you a Boy Scout?"

"I used to be. I'm going in again soon," Jimmy said.

"All right then. Scout's honor you will never go into the street to sell papers."

"On my honor as a Scout," Jimmy said.

Mr. Blackburn took Jimmy to the circulation department to get him started on his business career. "Do you have your father's permission?" he asked.

"Well —" Jimmy hesitated. "My father isn't living, and Mother didn't say 'Yes' right out, but I'm sure she will let me."

"Then we can't go ahead with this."

"You mean I don't get the job?" Jimmy sounded very disappointed. Mr. Blackburn shook his head. "Not without your mother's permission, young man. Get her to come down with you," he suggested, "and if it is okay with her I'll see that you get started right."

"Thank you, sir," Jimmy said, and added, "Gee, I was lucky running into you!"

That evening Jimmy talked to his mother. She was not at all convinced, but finally agreed to discuss things with Mr. Blackburn.

The following Saturday Jimmy and his mother were shown into the business manager's office.

"I started out as a newsboy," Mr. Blackburn told Mrs. Carter, "just as many of our successful businessmen have."

"But Jimmy wouldn't fit into the newspaper business, would he?" she asked.

"Oh, I'm not going to stick to it, Mom," Jimmy answered. "I've got other plans."

"What do you plan to be?" Mr. Blackburn asked Jimmy.

"I was going to play professional ball until this happened," Jimmy said. "Now I think I'll study law."

"Law?" Mr. Blackburn asked.

"My Dad was a lawyer," Jimmy said, "and I found out at the guide-dog school that there are a lot of successful lawyers who are blind."

Mr. Blackburn smiled at Mrs. Carter. "With your permission, we'll set Jimmy up in business. I have his promise, Scout's honor, that he will not go into the street to make sales." Then he turned to Jimmy. "You can't dispute the right of way with an automobile, Jimmy."

"No, sir. I wouldn't challenge his two hundred horsepower with my one dog-power. I'll stay on the sidewalk."

The final arrangements were made, and Jimmy and Leader were established with a newsstand, where Jimmy sold the evening paper after school hours and on Saturday afternoons.

Jimmy knew that he was working for his merit badges by earning money and conducting a business of his own. But there was one very important thing that all this did not provide. Jimmy loved the outdoors; he had been successful in baseball, athletics, and other outdoor games. Now he must find something to fill this need — something to bring him back into the group, to be a part of it, if not its leader.

Chapter
SIXTEEN

JIMMY COULDN'T UNDERSTAND what was the matter with Leader while they were at the newsstand. Leader never behaved like that before. He would occasionally lunge forward the full length of his leash, growling a very threatening growl. Jimmy would scold Leader and make him come back and lie down. This happened several times during each month, and Jimmy could not find out what was going on.

Carolyn often had to come to tell Jimmy it was time to go home for the evening meal.

"I'll have to move your bed out to your newsstand," his mother told him one evening.

"I don't want to live there, Mom, but it is a lot of fun and I'm making money." He emptied the money out of his pockets and Carolyn helped him count it. She, too, was proud of him.

"There's only one thing that worries me, Mom," Jimmy said.

"What's that, son?"

"There's a dog or something in that neighborhood bothering Leader. He growls and tries to get at it. That isn't like him. He's always gentle."

"Want me to come and see what it is?" Carolyn offered. "I could chase it."

"Thanks, Midget. But it probably isn't serious, and you wouldn't know when to be there. I guess we can work it out. Now I've got to hurry and get dressed before the fellows get here."

"Where are you going?" Carolyn asked.

"Scout meeting. You won't mind me not wiping the dishes, will you? It is my first meeting since — since — the accident."

"Good excuse," Carolyn grumbled.

"Don't complain, Carolyn," their mother said. "These men must have their lodge night. I'll help you."

Jimmy dashed to his room, and had just finished dressing when Chuck came by for him. "Art said he'd be late and would go right to the hut. We'll meet him there," he explained.

"We have to bring our packs, don't we?" Jimmy asked.

"Yeah, it's inspection, getting ready for our first cookout of the summer, now that school is over," Chuck answered.

"Well, I'm ready," said Jimmy, feeling to see if his hair was combed. "I'll get my pack. First chance to use my new equipment."

"Sure you've got everything?" Chuck asked. "Want me to check?"

"Haven't time," Jimmy answered. "Carolyn helped me. She read the list and I checked everything. I think it's all right." The two boys started for the meeting.

Chuck stopped him at the hut door. "Wait a minute, Jimmy. Mike is here."

"Good," said Jimmy. "I want to talk to him."

Chuck grabbed his arm. "Don't be a sap! It will mean trouble."

Leader gave a low growl. "Quiet, Leader," Jimmy said. "Chuck wasn't going to hurt me."

"Why, shame on you, Leader!" Chuck bent down to pat the dog. "Were you growling at me?"

Leader reached up to lick Chuck's face, then turned to look steadily at Mike.

"The Scoutmaster is coming toward us, Jimmy," Chuck whispered.

"Glad to see you, Carter," Mr. Douglas said. He guided Jimmy to a chair and helped him lay out his pack. Every piece of equipment had to be put in its proper place. Each boy stood by his open pack, and the Scoutmaster made the rounds, checking for any missing articles. Hank Saunders had brought his toothpaste but forgot his toothbrush. Joe neglected to bring a towel but brought a cake of soap.

When Mr. Douglas spoke to Chuck, Jimmy knew that he would be next. "Please, sir," Jimmy said quietly as he heard Mr. Douglas stop in front of him. "I would like to speak to Mike Adams."

Chuck stepped forward quickly. "Don't let him do it, sir. There's bad feeling between them."

"And you want to make up, Carter?" The Scoutmaster had heard Chuck, but paid no attention.

"Yes, sir," Jimmy answered.

"Well, that's fine. I congratulate you." He took Jimmy by the arm and led him to the center of the floor, with Jimmy holding Leader on leash.

"Adams," Mr. Douglas called. All the boys were watching. "I understand there's been a disagreement between you and Carter," the Scoutmaster went on. "He would like to shake hands with you. Come here. I want you two to make up."

Mike looked helplessly around the room. He didn't know what to do. He looked at the Scoutmaster, at Jimmy, and at Leader.

"Come ahead," Mr. Douglas commanded. "We can't have enmity in the troop, and if Carter makes the first offer, you should respond."

"Sure, Mike," Jimmy said. "I want to talk to you. I'd like to be friends." He held out his hand, but was facing in a different direction from where Mike was standing.

There was nothing Mike could do. Hesitantly he took a couple of steps toward Jimmy. Then he stopped and again looked around the room. Every boy was watching him. He clamped his jaws tight and started slowly toward Jimmy, anger and resentment boiling in him.

Leader didn't move. He didn't growl as Mike approached, but the hackles on the back of his neck rose, and his ears were pressed back tight against his head. He stood poised like an animal ready to leap upon its prey.

"I want you both to shake hands," the Scoutmaster said. "Whatever has happened must—" but that was as far as he got.

Mike was within reach of Leader's leash. All the pent-up anger came alive in Leader; all the days when Mike had teased him and kept just out of reach, and all the dog's desire to get at his tormentor, were crowded into

that one lunge. Leader leaped at Mike and sank his teeth in the calf of Mike's leg. He had not made a sound, no warning bark or growl, just the swift lunge and bite.

Mike screamed, half in pain, half in terror. He turned and rushed out of the room. Confusion followed. Everyone was talking at once.

Mr. Douglas felt responsible for the boys in his troop and took a serious view of what had happened. The dog had bitten one of his boys — without reason or provocation, as far as he could see. He dismissed the troop and went to Mike Adams' home to see how badly he was hurt.

Chuck and Art walked home with Jimmy and Leader. Jimmy was protesting all the way home. "*Leader is not a mean dog,*" he insisted. "There must be some mistake. He's never bitten anybody."

"But he did bite Mike in the leg," Chuck told him.

"It may have looked like it," Jimmy argued, "but Leader doesn't bite. He likes everybody."

"Yeah," said Chuck. "Leader liked Mike so well he tried to eat him." Chuck and Art laughed.

"That's not funny, and I don't care what anyone says. Leader is a good dog."

Leader walked along, his ears drooping sadly, his tail between his legs.

"Funny it should have been Mike," Chuck said as they turned into the path at Jimmy's home. "You wouldn't bite me, would you, Leader?" he added.

Leader looked up at him. His ears came up and his tail wagged feebly a couple of times, as if in thanks for the note of confidence in Chuck's voice; then his ears went down and his tail went between his legs again. The boys left and Jimmy went into the house to tell his mother and Carolyn what had happened.

They were still discussing the incident when Mr. Douglas arrived. "The Adams boy is severely bitten," he told Mrs. Carter as they joined Carolyn and Jimmy in the living room.

"Jimmy has been telling us about it," Mrs. Carter said, "and I can't understand it. The dog has always been so gentle."

"I had the doctor look at young Adams," Mr. Douglas said, "and of course we have to notify the Health Department."

"Health Department! Isn't Mike healthy?" Jimmy asked. "I mean, except for the bite?"

"You don't understand," Mr. Douglas explained. "The law requires that your dog must be quarantined."

"Quarantined for what?" Jimmy asked. "Leader isn't sick."

"Probably not," Mr. Douglas said, "but he must be kept in the house, off the street, and away from people for fourteen days."

"Fourteen days! That's crazy. If he can't go out, I'd be the same as in jail," Jimmy protested.

"No, you won't be quarantined. It's the dog," Mr. Douglas told him.

"Carolyn will be with you, now that school's over," his mother suggested. "She won't mind."

"How about my paper corner?" Jimmy asked. "She can't stay with me there."

"Sure, Jimmy. I can help you sell papers," Carolyn said.

"And who will stay with Leader? Can't leave him alone," Jimmy argued.

"I didn't make the law, Carter, and there is nothing I can do about it." Mr. Douglas was emphatic.

"I'm sure we can work it out, Jimmy," his mother said.

"The health officer will be here in the morning, and you can talk to him." Mr. Douglas rose to go.

Early the next morning the health officer arrived and put Leader under quarantine, while Jimmy protested indignantly that the whole thing was an outrage.

Chuck and Art had difficulty persuading their parents that it was safe to visit Jimmy while Leader was under suspicion of being a vicious dog. Other people took sides in the argument, and Mike enjoyed being the center of the conflict.

Carolyn came in one evening, her clothing torn and muddy.

"For goodness sake, Carolyn," her mother exclaimed, "what on earth have you been doing?"

"I had a fight, Mommy, and I'm glad of it," sobbed Carolyn. "You can't scold me for it either."

"Not until I know what it's all about. Why were you fighting?"

"They said Leader was a dangerous dog and ought to be shot!" Carolyn was getting angry all over again. "I had to fight 'em, didn't I, Mommy?"

"No, you didn't have to, but I won't scold you."

"Thanks, Midget," Jimmy said. "You know Leader isn't vicious."

"But I'm afraid Carolyn is." Their mother smiled. "They'll quarantine you, dear, if you aren't careful."

"Mom, they can't shoot Leader, can they?" Jimmy just realized what Carolyn had said. "Do something, Mom!" he added frantically. "We've got to do something. They can't, Mom, they can't!" Jimmy had half risen from his chair.

"Now, don't get excited, Jimmy. I don't think it will go that far," his mother said quietly. "We know Leader is gentle, and there must have been some reason for what he did."

"Can we go to the Health Department?" Jimmy asked. "Let them see Leader. That will prove it."

"That may not be necessary, but I would like to know how badly Mike is hurt," she answered.

"Gee, I never thought of that, Mom. Do you think he's hurt bad?" Then he added quietly, "Now I've done something to him the way he did to me."

Mrs. Carter looked at her son with loving understanding.

"Could you take me to see him sometime, Mom, and let me tell him I'm sorry for what Leader did?" Jimmy went on.

"I'm glad you want to go, Jimmy. Mrs. Adams came to me when you were hurt, and I would like you to go and see them now."

Mrs. Carter went to the telephone and called Mrs. Adams. She explained Jimmy's request, and Mrs. Adams was very glad to have them come.

They went that same evening, Carolyn staying at home with Leader. Mrs. Adams met them at the door. "Come in," she said. "Mike is in the living room." She put her arm affectionately around Jimmy.

"Hello, Mrs. Adams," said Jimmy. "Is Mike's leg very bad?"

"I'm afraid his feelings are hurt worse than his leg, but you ask him. Mike!" she called. "Here's Jimmy come to see you." She led Jimmy into the room.

"Hi, Mike!" said Jimmy.

In the presence of Mrs. Carter and his mother and with the absence of Leader, Mike felt secure. "Hi," he answered from the other end of the room.

"I've been wanting to talk to you, Mike, for a long time."

"Yeah?" Mike asked, not knowing just what Jimmy wanted to talk about.

"Yes," Jimmy answered. "I wanted to tell you that I know you didn't throw that firecracker at me on purpose. It was an accident, and I'm not mad about it."

Mike's eyes opened wide. He swallowed once and tried to speak. He hadn't expected this. "You mean you're not sore at me any more?" he stammered.

"No, Mike. I'd like for us to be friends again. I tried to tell you at the Scout meeting."

The two women looked at each other. Mrs. Carter crossed over to Jimmy and slipped her arm through his.

Mrs. Adams smiled. "I've got some cake in the kitchen, and I thought I might make some lemonade. Want to help me, Mrs. Carter?"

"I certainly do," said Mrs. Carter, taking the hint, and they left the two boys alone in the room.

"I thought you were sore at me," Mike said slowly. "The rest of the gang wouldn't have anything to do with me, and I thought you put them up to it."

"But I didn't," said Jimmy. "I might have been sore at first, but I've learned that when you hate someone you are carrying poison around with you, and I don't want to hate anybody."

"I hated you, Jimmy," Mike said seriously.

"But you don't now, do you?" Jimmy asked. "And I'm sorry for what Leader did to you."

"And I'm sorry for what I did to you," Mike said.

Jimmy held out his hand. "I guess neither one of us could help it."

"There's something I have to tell you, Jimmy," Mike said slowly.

"Yeah? What?"

"It wasn't Leader's fault he bit me," Mike began.

"What do you mean?" Jimmy asked.

"I — I — well, I've been teasing him. The first time I saw him and you going home from school I slapped at him kinda in play and he growled at me, and that made me sore because I was sore at you. Then when you were selling papers on the corner, every time I passed I teased him."

"Oh, that's what was the matter with him!" Jimmy exclaimed. "I wondered what made him act like that. I thought it was another dog."

"It was me," Mike said, getting the whole story off his chest. "I made him mad at me, and when I got near him at the Scout meeting he bit me. I — I guess I had it coming, Jimmy. Then when everybody felt sorry for me — oh, I don't know — I guess I just got all mixed up."

"Mack said you can't be happy until you quit hating," Jimmy said quietly.

"What's that?" asked Mike.

"Oh, nothing. I was just thinking of my roommate at the guide-dog school."

"Tell me about the school, Jimmy. What's it like?"

And Jimmy, glad of a fresh audience, told the whole story of Leader and their training.

When the two mothers came back with the lemonade and cake the boys were deep in friendly conversation, and the past was forgotten.

"Mom," Jimmy said. "Mike just told me why Leader bit him."

"Do you have to tell, Jim?" Mike asked.

"Don't you want me to? If we don't, they might shoot Leader."

"Shoot him!" said Mike. "But they can't! He's a swell dog."

"They say he's vicious," Jimmy explained. "And you've got to save him."

"Okay," said Mike. "I guess you better tell 'em, but I kinda hate to."

"I knew there was some good reason," Mrs. Carter said after they had told the story to her. "We must phone the Scoutmaster and let him set the record straight."

"Does everybody have to know it?" Mike protested. "I'll be in the doghouse again."

"We'll just tell the Scoutmaster, and he can explain to the Health Department," said Mrs. Carter. "No one else needs to know."

"And I can save Leader from getting shot!" Mike's shoulders straightened and his chin came up as he said it.

"If you boys go to the Scout meeting together," Mrs. Adams suggested, "I think the rest of the boys will soon fall in line."

"What about Leader?" Mike asked. "He doesn't like me."

"You'll have to make up with him slowly, Mike," Jimmy said. "I think when he knows we're friends he'll get to like you."

"Yeah, but I can't get near him." Mike was doubtful.

"I'll let Chuck hold him while you and I shake hands and show him that we're friends. I think he'll let you make up. He's a smart dog, Mike. He's just got more sense!"

"I know he's smart," said Mike. "I wish I had a dog like him."

The Scoutmaster explained to the Health Department, but the quarantine had to run the full course prescribed by law. As soon as it was lifted, the Scoutmaster called the pack inspection meeting that had been interrupted.

Mike and Leader got acquainted with each other all over again. Leader was on guard, not quite sure yet, but he accepted Mike with no outward show of resentment. The troop also accepted the situation, and with true Boy Scout spirit forgave and very quickly forgot.

The Scoutmaster watched Jimmy lay out his pack for inspection. Jimmy had memorized accurately the location for each article and was able to check his equipment without help.

He had passed that test, but now he must show that he could keep up with the troop on a hike.

Chapter
SEVENTEEN

THE TROOP GATHERED at the Boy Scout hut for an early-morning start. Each Scout was carrying his pack and equipment for the overnight camping trip. They were to make a two-and-a-half hour hike into the hills before they stopped for lunch, and then go on to their campsite.

As the sun rose higher, the rough trail grew steeper. It was different from the sidewalks on which Jimmy and Leader had trained. In some places the trail was very narrow. It was wide enough for the boys walking single file, but with Leader at his side Jimmy was scratched by the underbrush. The other boys could step over the little gullies, but Jimmy stepped into them. He stumbled over the loose stones, slipping and sliding. Leader tried frantically to guide him. He would tug at the harness to pull Jimmy to one side, and the next instant throw his weight against Jimmy's leg to guide him around a small boulder. Leader was panting, his tongue dripping. He strained beside his master as Jimmy struggled on.

The pack was growing unbearably heavy, and Jimmy felt he could not go much farther. Then he heard the Scoutmaster's whistle call a halt. Jimmy slipped off his pack and dropped to the ground, Leader lying close beside him and both of them breathing heavily. The rest of the Scouts hurried around, gathering wood for the fire.

After lunch and a short rest, they continued up the hill. This part of the trail was smoother and wider, allowing Leader to walk beside Jimmy and guide him as he would on a broken sidewalk. The troop was able to make better progress, and they reached their campsite by late afternoon. The rest of the day was spent in making camp for the night.

Some of the boys helped Jimmy make up his sleeping bag.

"Try that out, Jimmy," said Mike. "I think it's all right."

"Where'd you put the box springs?" Jimmy asked, squirming a little on the hard ground.

"Did you say box or rocks?" Mike asked.

"Same thing," said Chuck. "You'll sleep on 'em."

He was right. After a dinner of beans, roasted wieners, and toasted marshmallows, followed by a few sleepy campfire songs, the boys turned in.

Leader curled up as close to Jimmy as he could without crawling into the sleeping bag with him. Everyone slept. Leader joined in the chorus of soft breathing that blended with the soft sounds of the night.

Suddenly Jimmy tried to sit up, but his sleeping bag held him like a straitjacket. He thought he was having another dream until his head bumped against the ground and he came fully awake. Even then it took a few seconds to realize where he was. When Jimmy moved, Leader woke, stood up, stretched, flapped his ears, and rattled his chain collar, then came over to lick Jimmy's face,

In stretching and shaking, Leader had walked over Chuck, who was sleeping next to Jimmy. Chuck rubbed his eyes and looked around.

"Hey, Jimmy," he whispered. "Go back to sleep."

"Oh, is it still night?" Jimmy asked. "Day noises and night noises are the same up here."

"Quiet!" Chuck advised. "You'll wake up the gang."

"Is the sun shining?" Jimmy whispered back.

"No, it's just getting daylight. Hey! It's almost sunrise. You gave me an idea." Chuck crawled out of his bag and went over to Art and then to Mike. "What do you fellows say to going up that hill to see the sunrise?" he suggested, pointing.

"Sure," they agreed.

"Okay. Be quiet though," cautioned Chuck.

"Anyone else awake?" Art whispered.

"Just Jimmy. He woke me," Chuck whispered back.

"Want to take him along?" asked Art.

"That's a gag," said Chuck. "What fun would Jimmy have going to look at a sunrise?"

"He'd go for the walk," Art explained.

"Yeah, Leader might like to see the sunrise." Mike looked over to where the dog was standing, his front paws on Jimmy's sleeping bag.

Again in whispers they explained the excursion to Jimmy.

"Sure," said Jimmy. "Now that I'm awake I don't want to miss any of the fun you fellows are having."

"Well, hurry up then," Chuck urged.

"Okay." Jimmy slid out of his sleeping bag, quickly

dressed, and harnessed Leader. Then the group quietly went over to the highest hill.

They stood in awe at the majesty of the sunrise, the red glow followed by streamers of bright gold. Then the disk of sun, like molten fire, peeked over the top of the distant hills.

"It's wonderful!" Chuck said quietly. "Wish you could see it, Jimmy."

"I can see it without looking." Jimmy grinned. "And I wouldn't have to come up here to do that."

"Hey, fellows!" Mike suggested. "Want to see the sunrise twice in the same day?"

"I can see it rise half a dozen times a day," Jimmy said.

"No, I mean it," Mike insisted. "If we go into the valley down there, we'll see the sun come up over those near hills for a second sunrise."

"I wonder," said Chuck. "But it would be daylight, wouldn't it?"

"It's daylight now," said Art.

"But it isn't down there in the valley. Look!" said Mike.

"Let's try it," Chuck agreed. "We can get back before breakfast."

They started down the hill into the valley, intent upon watching for the first glimpse of the sun.

"Hey, there it is!" Chuck exclaimed. "Mike was right. It's coming up again, twice in the same day."

Art just stood and stared, while Mike smiled proudly.

After a while the boys decided to return to camp. "Which way do we go?" Chuck asked. "There's no trail down here."

"I think this is the hill we came over." Mike pointed to a hill on their right.

"No, we came down toward our left," Art said. "That would be south, so we will have to go back toward the north."

They argued over the directions until they realized they were completely lost.

"We can't be far from camp," Mike insisted. "It's just over the hill."

"Yeah, but which hill? The farther we walk, the farther we may go from the camp," Chuck argued.

"I'm sorry, fellows. I got you into this," said Mike. "I never thought we could get lost."

"I guess the best thing would be to stay here and let them find us," Chuck decided.

"No," Art argued. "We don't know how soon they will miss us, and we might miss breakfast."

"We have no water and no equipment. We can't stay here," Mike pointed out.

"Who's got a compass, and which way should we go?" Chuck asked.

"Well," Art said, "the sun's in the east."

"Yeah, the sun's in the east, and we're in a valley and we're lost," Mike added. "I don't mind telling you I'm worried."

"So am I," put in Chuck. Jimmy had been listening quietly. He remembered when he got lost at the guide-dog school, but now there was no Mr. Weeks to send a pair of high heels to his rescue.

"Look, fellows," he said. "All three of you want to go in a different direction. You admit we are lost."

"Yeah," Mike said. "I guess we are."

"Then will you let me try something? We can't be more lost."

"What can you do?" Chuck asked impatiently.

"If you'll trust me I'll show you," Jimmy said confidently.

"Okay," Art said, "let him try. Maybe he can see things we can't."

"All right," the others agreed. "Which way, Jimmy?"

For answer Jimmy took hold of the handle on Leader's harness and said firmly, "Leader, take me home. Home, Leader!"

The dog looked up at Jimmy and wagged his tail as if he understood, and then started straight for a hill that none of them had chosen.

"That can't be right," Mike protested. "He's taking us wrong."

"You said you'd trust me," Jimmy insisted. "I told Leader to take me home. He can't take me to my real home, but I bet he takes me where we slept last night. You wait and see."

The boys started up the hill, slipping and sliding at every step. It hadn't seemed that steep when they came down. They were getting more worried, more frightened as they climbed.

"Hey, this is crazy!" Chuck sputtered. "Are we gonna follow the dog if he chases a rabbit? I know we're wrong!"

"But do you know which is right?" Jimmy countered.

"Let's go on," Mike advised. "We can see and be seen better at the top."

"I agree with Chuck," said Art. "Let's stop and look around."

"You fellows do the looking. I believe Leader knows what he's doing. I'm going on." Jimmy climbed steadily beside his dog. The boys reluctantly followed, complaining more loudly as fear gripped them and the realization of their situation came over them, but they continued up the hill.

"Look!" Chuck suddenly shouted, and he pointed straight ahead.

"What is it?" Jimmy asked.

"Well, what do you know!" said Mike. "It's a column of smoke rising as straight as an Indian signal."

"Must be the breakfast campfire," Art added. "And boy, am I hungry!"

They rush on up the hill. "Hey, fellows!" Jimmy called to them. "That's not fair! Leader found the way and you gotta let him lead us in."

"You're right, Jimmy," Chuck admitted, and the boys dropped back, single file, behind their guide, marching into camp.

"Where have you fellows been?" the Scoutmaster scolded. "You were absent without permission."

"Just over the hill." Chuck explained how they had seen a double sunrise, and how the east side of the hill looked different with the changing shadows.

"We got lost and Leader led us into camp," Art put in.

"Then Leader will be excused," Mr. Douglas said. "The rest of you will be held to account at our next meeting. You know you should be punished."

"I'm afraid it's my fault, sir. I suggested it," said Mike.

"That will be up to the patrol," the Scoutmaster answered. "Now I suggest you get your mess kits for breakfast. Of course this will not happen again!"

"Oh no, sir!" the four answered in chorus.

The story of their getting lost spread quickly through the group. Each boy had the only correct explanation of how Leader found his way back to camp.

"He smelled the smoke from our fire," one of the boys explained.

"He just followed their scent on the back track," another Scout told them. "That's easy."

"More likely he smelled the food," said a third.

"Why can't you believe the truth?" Jimmy protested. "I told him to take me home and he did it."

Whatever the explanation, Leader had won the respect of all. Jimmy took off Leader's harness, allowing him to be just a dog, instead of a guide dog, and the boys gathered around him. Then Jimmy unhooked the leash and Leader was free to romp over the hills, to chase and be chased by the boys, but he never got very far from Jimmy and never took his attention from his master for long.

After breakfast and cleaning up the camp, the boys went over to the stream to try to catch some fish for lunch. Jimmy felt awkward because he had not tried to fish since he lost his sight. The Scoutmaster showed him how to reel in his line as far as it would go, follow the pole to the end, and then slide the line through his fingers carefully until he came to the hook. In this way he could avoid any accident to himself or to others.

The boys were clustered more or less in one short

stretch along the bank of the stream, but Jimmy moved to a spot away from them, so there would be no chance of hooking one of them when he cast.

Jimmy's training since he had become blind had taught him to be alert, to listen, and to react to everything that went on around him. No fish that nibbled at his hook would steal the bait and get away!

They fished awhile, and some of the boys, including Jimmy, caught a few fish — but the fish were not biting freely. It was warm on the bank in the sun, and the water seemed cool so the boys got permission to put on their trunks and go swimming.

Jimmy folded his clothes neatly, stuffed his socks inside his shoes, and placed them on top of his things. With his clothes stacked in this way, Jimmy could recognize them when he finished swimming. Then he put Leader on guard.

Leader didn't like this idea at all. He sat by Jimmy's clothes until he saw Jimmy going near the edge of the bank. Orders may be orders, but Leader knew his duty; he also knew when orders must be disobeyed. In three bounds he was in front of Jimmy with his ribs pressed against Jimmy's shins, blocking the path and barking a warning.

Jimmy knelt down and hugged the dog. "It's all right, Leader," he explained. "I know what I'm doing," and he sent Leader back to stay with his clothes.

He had to scold Leader a little, but finally made the dog understand that he must obey. He sat on the bank awhile, just to satisfy Leader, before he eased himself into the water, calling to the dog all the time, "Stay, Leader. Sit, Leader. Stay!"

The water was comfortably cool, and Jimmy found he could swim as well as he ever had. He kept with the other boys, having a wonderful time and finding no reason to be afraid. When he wanted to stand up and rest, he found the water over his head. He hadn't thought to ask how deep it was, and now he was not sure of the direction of shallow water.

He trod water for a few minutes as he called to one of the boys near him, "Hey, which direction is the shallow water? Which way is the bank?"

"A little to your left, Jimmy," Chuck said as he swam closer to him. "I'd say about ten o'clock. Follow me. Got the direction of my voice?"

"Yeah," said Jimmy, "if you keep talking. With all this noise it seems to echo from all directions."

Chuck paced Jimmy in toward shore. "You've got nerve, Jimmy. I don't believe I'd try to swim if I couldn't see."

"It's not a matter of nerve — it's the only way I can swim if I want to swim." Jimmy grinned and added, "Thanks, Chuck." As Jimmy climbed up on the bank he was met by the Scoutmaster and Leader.

"I've been watching you, Carter," Mr. Douglas said. "I think you're getting along fine."

"Thank you, sir."

Leader didn't say anything, but he'd been watching too, and he wasn't so pleased at what Jimmy had been doing. He came up and licked Jimmy's hand.

Jimmy took hold of the harness. "I told you to guard my clothes, Leader. Now find my clothes."

Mr. Douglas smiled as he stood watching. "I'll show you where they are, Carter."

Leader started off briskly toward the little pile of Jimmy's clothes. "I'll be all right," Jimmy called back.

The smile slowly left the Scoutmaster's face. He too looked at Leader with respect and admiration. "I wouldn't have believed it," he said to Jimmy as he turned away.

Jimmy took a brisk rubdown and started to put on his clothes. The air seemed thick with the shouts and laughter of the boys who were still swimming. Then Jimmy's attentive ears caught a new note. Leader, too, sprang to his feet, alert, with a short bark; then they both

heard it again. It was a distinct cry for help, though muffled as if whoever had made it had taken a mouthful of water. It sounded like Mike, but Jimmy could not be sure, with the distorted tone and the conflict of other noises. Whoever it was, he was in trouble. Jimmy took a step forward, pointing in the direction of the sound. "Go get him, Leader!" he commanded sharply.

Jimmy was calling on the instinct of the shepherd dog to protect the flock, handed down through countless generations. "Fetch, Leader!" Jimmy repeated, swinging his arm. Like a shot the dog was off. He splashed into the water and swam out straight to the sound of the voice.

"There's someone in trouble," Jimmy shouted to the Scoutmaster, who had not distinguished the one sound among all the others.

Mr. Douglas blew his whistle, bringing silence. Several of the older boys, following the direction in which the Scoutmaster was pointing, swam the short distance to where Leader was trying to keep his nose above water while Mike clung to his harness.

Together they got Mike up onto the bank and massaged the calf of his leg where the cramp had caught him, while Leader danced about, proud and happy in his achievement, then shook himself violently, giving the boys a shower bath.

"Hey, Leader, you'll drown me all over again," Mike laughed shakily. Leader cocked his head, looked at Mike for a moment, then went over to him and licked his face. The boy threw his arms around the dog and hugged him. All suspicion melted away in their newly found friendship.

"Are you all right, Adams?" the Scoutmaster asked.

"Yes, sir. Just a cramp. I guess I got scared."

"It's a good thing you called, and it's a good thing Carter and his dog heard you."

"Yes, sir!" Mike said as he sat up. "He's the most wonderful dog in the world. That's twice he saved me today."

"Yes," agreed Mr. Douglas heartily. "He *is* a wonderful dog."

When the boys found that Mike was all right, they dashed back to their clothes, racing to see who would get dressed first and who would be the "rotten egg."

Like a troop of wild Indians, they headed for the campsite and lunch. After lunch they broke camp and headed for home.

"Let me carry your pack, Jimmy," Mike suggested as Jimmy's feet slid occasionally over the rough ground.

"I can carry it," Jimmy protested.

"But it's harder to keep your balance going downhill," Mike insisted, wanting an excuse to be near Leader.

"Carter," the Scoutmaster interrupted. "The boys want to know more about how your dog works. I'd like you to tell us about him at the next meeting."

"Sure," said Jimmy, glad of the prospect of a new audience for the story of Leader's accomplishments.

At the next Scout meeting, the four boys were called up for discipline, but the patrol was inclined to be lenient.

Then the Scoutmaster asked Jimmy to give his talk. Jimmy told them that Leader's registered name was Sirius, for the Dog Star. He told of the training at the school, and explained that no one must pet or interfere with a guide dog while it is working.

"Leader can go with me into hotels and restaurants," Jimmy continued. "He could go into swanky places where I might get chased out." The boys laughed.

"He's just a part of me," Jimmy added. "I guess we're Siamese twins." He reached down to stroke Leader.

After Jimmy's talk, the Scoutmaster complimented him on all he had accomplished, reminding the patrol that in spite of his blindness Jimmy was going to public school, selling newspapers and making money at it, and now had kept up with the best of them on a campout with the troop.

"Carter," the Scoutmaster continued, "has been going

through a long, dark corridor. Now he has come out of it and is living a normal, useful life, asking no favors and doing his share of whatever is to be done. The patrol can be proud to have a boy like Carter as a member. And as for Leader," he went on, "I think he deserves an honorary lifesaving award."

The boys clapped and cheered.

Leader, sitting on his haunches next to Jimmy, barked at the noise as if he also approved the suggestion.

"Carter, we will let you present the award." Mr. Douglas brought Jimmy a wide piece of blue ribbon. "Put this around the dog's neck, and you can demonstrate how good you are at tying a butterfly bow."

Leader sat like a statue while Jimmy tied the ribbon and the boys again applauded.

"Sir!" Mike spoke up when the noise had subsided. "I move that we adopt Leader as our mascot and that we change our name to the Dog Star Patrol."

The boys greeted this proposal with more and louder cheers, and the motion was passed with enthusiasm.

When the meeting was over, Jimmy got to his feet, and the boys crowded around, all wanting to pat their new mascot. Leader stood quietly, his slowly waving tail showing his pleasure in their attentions. But after a few minutes he moved over to lean against Jimmy's legs, and nudged his nose gently into Jimmy's palm, as if to remind the boys that he had work to do.

Jimmy laughed and bent down to fondle the dog's ears. "That's right, Leader," he said, "it's time we went home."

He took hold of the handle on Leader's harness and

said to his friends, "He'll make a swell mascot in his spare time, but he knows his main job is being four-legged eyes for me."

Then, turning toward the door, with a wide smile and a cheerful wave of his free hand, Jimmy gave the command: "Forward!"